THE LUNAR
FREEDOM
REBELLION

THE LUNAR FREEDOM REBELLION

T LAWTON CARNEY

Queer Space

New Orleans

Published in the United States of America by
Queer Space
A Rebel Satori Imprint
www.rebelsatoripress.com

Paperback ISBN: 978-1-60864-219-9
Ebook ISBN: 978-1-60864-220-5

CONTENTS

For Robert

From Terra to Luna

"*The moon, by her comparative proximity, and the constantly vary-ing appearances produced by her several phases, has always occupied a considerable share of the attention of the inhabitants of the Earth.*"

—Jules Verne, From the Earth to the Moon

CHAPTER ONE

Jason Escobar stepped out of the gravlift onto the hotel's pool patio forty-six stories above the city of Palm Springs, Area 22, Earth. The bar, on the far side of the patio, was a pool of light and numerous people were sitting on the stools that abutted the stainless steel and plascrete fixture. Jason selected a stool with no one on either side and sat down. The droidtender arrived and began wiping the bar with a small cloth.

"What will you have, sir?"

"A Cerillion brandy, please,"

The droid whirled around and headed to the other end of the bar. Jax turned on the barstool and surveyed the crowd. To his right, a woman dressed in the latest style of asteroid dress threw him a broad smile and moved provocatively on the stool. Before he could turn away, she said,

"How are you, big boy?"

Jax almost laughed out loud but answered after he had swallowed the laugh that threatened to come out,

"On a beautiful evening like this how could anyone be anything but well and happy."

"Oh, I can think of a lot of reasons one could be happy. If you take me to your room we might find out."

"Only if you bring your brother along," Jason said, this time with a small smile."

"Enjoy the evening," he added and turned to his left.

There, a man of about thirty-five years old with blond hair and an almost pudgy figure sat staring at the eastern hills beyond Palm Springs. He was dressed in clothes that were about five years outdated and before Jax could turn away he said,

"It's a beautiful evening out there, isn't it?"

"It sure is. I was up here earlier watching the moon rise. It's full tonight, you know." Jax replied. The man turned to Jax and said,

"Don't I know. I begin my return there tomorrow on the 09:00 shuttle from Blythe," he said.

"I'm on the 15:00 shuttle. What do you do up there?"

"I work for the miner's union. I've been here in a conference with the heads of various departments within the main offices of the Lunar Management Company," he replied.

"How have your talks been going?"

"Like all meetings, we agree on some things but not how safety in the mines is being addressed," Chuck said. "The meetings were far ranging. Mars, Phobos, Titan as well as the moon are in jeopardy. What will you be doing on the Moon?"

"I'll be working in management. But tell me, what makes you believe there are problems with the reporting on the accidents?"

"Look at the reports on the decompression accident last year that killed over one hundred men and women working in the largest mine in the solar system near Luna City."

"The reports I've seen made it clear there was no fault on the part of LMC. It was the catastrophic failure of one of those locks that created the sudden decompression which sucked the workers to their deaths on the lunar regolith."

The man looked at Jason for a moment then said,

"I'm here to enjoy myself and take my mind away from those challenges until my return to Luna. My name is Charlemagne Breckman. My friends call me Chuck."

"I'm Jason Escobar and my friends call me Jax. As I said, I'm also on my way to the moon on tomorrow's 15:00 shuttle."

"Sorry we aren't on the same shuttle, but once on the moon, we'll have a lot to talk about if we get the chance. What kind of management work do you do that gets you to the moon?"

""I've been hired as the Level Six Administrator. I have an MA in municipal government and I wanted to go to the moon. Once in a lifetime and all that."

The look on Chuck's face said it all but the men were momentarily distracted by the light coming from the east.

The moon had now risen far enough above the low mountains to reach its spectacular and magnificent silver-white place in Earth's heavens as its lone satellite. Jason watched as a bright blaze of light appeared just above the mountains and rose into the sky leaving a hot white contrail that slashed in front of the moon as it floated serenely above the desert floor. A few moments later he felt and heard the muffled sonic boom of the liftoff.

"Man," said Chuck, "every ten minutes or so another one boosts for the heavens. What do you know about Blythe?"

""Not a whole lot. I've only been in space once and that was an orbital insertion to learn how to handle myself in zero gravity. We boosted from Blythe."

"Until it opened, this area was an underused piece of the planet, You know it's all owned by Lunar Management, don't you?"

"It's interesting I didn't know that."

"I believe you'll find out a lot they didn't tell you."

The importance of Blythe wasn't lost on Jax. He would depart tomorrow from Blythe to arrive at Delhi2, the largest space platform of three that functioned as a transfer point to the larger transports.

"LMC closed the last Earth-based mine two hundred years ago. The mines they have all over the cosmos bring in hundreds of trillions of credits for the company."

"Tonight, however, I would prefer to spend time enjoying the music and drinks here. Do you mind?" Breckman said.

"It's my last night on Earth for a long time and I'm just as happy talking about anything but the moon and its challenges," Jax answered with a smile.

Their conversation turned to the area around them, then sports, and finally the opportunities springing up all around the solar system for men and women looking for adventure and challenges beyond what was available on Earth. Inevitably the conversation turned, once again, to the planets and the moon in particular.

"The Earth can't continue to try to support the twenty billion people living here. . All the very best jobs are headed out to the planets. The moon has been a colony for more than two hundred and fifty years and at some point it, too, will have to limit the number of citizens able to successfully live on that sphere." Chuck said ruefully.

"I hadn't thought of that," said Jax. "LMC is opening their new South Pole-Aitken Basin mine soon. My research did reveal most of the housing is complete and they are now waiting for the maglev to be completed."

"But, you know all that, don't you, Chuck?"

"Yeh, and its safety procedures and equipment tests are one of the things I was here to talk about at the company's headquarters. You're also wrong about the maglev, it was opened to traffic just last week. There will certainly be an increase in the activity out that way. Once we're back on the moon maybe you and I could meet sometime and talk about what you and your administrative team will be doing at the new mine. It's going to be larger than Tycho Base when fully operational." Chuck said.

"This is a new job for me and I can't commit to what I'll know or where I'll be stationed. I'll keep your concerns in mind, however. Goodnight, Chuck. Have safe travels tomorrow." Jax said as he stood and threw a fifty-credit plaque on the bar.

"Oh, don't leave. We could continue the conversation in your room or mine if you would like."

"Thanks, but no. I'm expecting a comm this evening and should return to my room. We'll meet on the moon soon enough." Jax said. Then added,

"The drinks are on me." And he left the bar. Chuck's attempt to get him alone wasn't lost on Jax. Not really my type, he thought as he headed for the gravlift. Still, his concerns were something Jax had heard during his hiring process. This was the first time he had been able to listen to someone put the matter in a way that was personal and urgent. It gave him a lot to think about over the next few days as he traveled to the moon.

Chuck, for his part, watched as Jax crossed the patio. He was dressed in a light blue open-collared shirt, beige slacks, and a black sports jacket; all of which enhanced his one-hundred eighty-five-pound body and well-muscled physic that was both attractive and, Chuck imagined, lethal. His dark brown hair was cut short and it helped frame a face and deep-set dark blue eyes that Chuck found pleasing. With a wistful smile, Chuck turned to the bar and his drink.

CHAPTER TWO

Jax crossed the pool patio to the gravlift and hopped aboard.

"Level ten," he said and started his descent. The lift took him to his floor without stopping and Jax stepped out of the tube and turned to his right. He had enjoyed his last evening on Earth and looked forward to relaxing in his room which had a view out over the valley to the same far mountains he had watched the moon come over earlier. He palmed the plate next to his room's door and with a hiss, it slid open. There was a light on next to the pair of tall pale green synthon fabric wing chairs that faced the windows and for a moment Jax was taken aback. It must have been the night chamber droid turning down the beds for the guests he thought. He began to remove his jacket as he walked toward the chairs.

"Come in, Mr. Escobar and have a seat." a disembodied voice said from one of the chairs facing the window. Jax quickly reached into his jacket for the lasgun he usually kept there, but the empty pocket reminded him he wasn't allowed to take it to the moon. and as he removed his empty hand the voice continued.

"Don't be frightened. I'm not here to hurt you but I do need to have a word. Sit down, sit down."

Jax moved to the opposite chair and sat as he had been told. He recognized the man from interviews during his hiring process. At that time the man had not spoken but Jax knew he was part of the management team. He was more curious than frightened and decided to let this person do all the talking.

Settled deep in the shadows of the chair was a man in his late thirties with dark black hair, skin the color of amber, and sparkling green eyes. Jax waited for what he had to say.

He reached into a pocket inside his tailored sky-blue light wool jacket and took out a tobacco stick.

"You don't mind if I smoke, do you?" he didn't wait for a reply and struck one end of the stick against the table to light it. As he drew on the stick Jax noticed his nails were painted a deep shade of magenta. Interesting, he thought. The man took a deep draw on the stick, let the smoke slowly pour from his full lips which were painted the same color as his nails, and gave Jax a long look.

"I am the personal private assistant to Mr. Joseph Warren, director of LMC and he has specific instructions for you and your new job. You will travel tomorrow as planned and when you reach the moon you will still report to Mr. Nkosi who will reassign you. You will be stationed at the new outpost at Aitken immediately and oversee the Infrastructure and Management Division. Mr. Nkosi will remain at Luna City and Tycho base, leaving you in complete charge of the Aitken facility. With this additional responsibility, we will, of course, increase your salary. Once you have arrived at Aitken and gotten acquainted with your team, I'll contact you with further instructions. Do you understand?" he said.

"Those were not my orders and how do I know you are who you say you are?"

"I'm Reginald Tebaldi, not that my name matters, and I handle all of Mr. Warren's private communications with complete discretion," he said as he passed a small ID plaque over to Jax to inspect. He took a look and returned it.

"Any time I speak to you I speak on behalf of Mr. Warren. Is that understood?"

"Okay, so you're his spokesperson. Why is he changing my orders and is Mr. Nkosi aware of the change? Also, is Mr. Warren still the senior manager of the Lunar Management Company Security Council?"

"He is, but it's not your business to question Mr. Warren's directions. You and a team of thirty men and women will create a strong security force. Your new team will enforce any orders that might come from Mr. Warren or me. Nkosi will be told what he needs to know and you will not share the communications we have with anyone else either here or on the moon. Again, is that understood?"

Jax was in a quandary. A brand-new job and the director of the board of the Security Council of the Lunar Management Company decides to order him personally to a new position on the moon without the knowledge of his immediate superior. Okay, now what?

"Is Nkosi okay with the transfer? Will he give me any trouble?" Jax asked.

"Nkosi is no concern of yours and there will be no trouble with your move to the Aitken outpost. Now, Mr. Escobar, it is time for me to leave. Do we have a complete understanding of your new position and Mr. Warren's control of that new post?" he said as he rose out of the shadows of the large chair.

Gad, thought Jax, he's beautiful. He was slender, about 5'8" tall, and dressed in the tailored jacket-pant suit now in fashion. The trousers were tight enough for Jax to see Tebaldi was very nicely endowed. It was all in complete contrast to the colored lips and nails. With it all, however, it almost took Jax's breath away.

"Well?" he said.

"Oh, yeah, I understand." he was able to stammer out.

8

"Good, you'll be hearing from me once you're in position on the moon. Until then remember, do not share this meeting with anyone."

He turned and walked across the room toward the door still wreathed in cigarette smoke. He stopped with his hand just over the access plaque.

"No one," he said and touched the plaque which opened the door. With one last look, he exited and Jax was left staring at the closed door.

CHAPTER THREE

Jax awoke the next morning after a fitful night in which he envisioned angry bosses and out-of-control team members. It was already 11:00 hours and it was later than he had planned. He quickly shaved, showered, and had a cup of jolt. He pulled on a crisp white shirt and a travel suit of dark blue trousers, and a pale fawn-colored short jacket. He closed the account for the hotel and made his way to the transit center for the short ride to Blythe Space Port.

He had pre-paid for his seat and was aboard five minutes before departure. Just before the maglev left the terminal a man sat down next to him.

"On your way to Blythe or destinations beyond?" he said.

"Blythe. And you?"

"I'm on my way to Chicago, via Denver. Are you staying on the platform or traveling to one of the planets?"

"Stopping at the moon."

At that moment the maglev accelerated out of the terminal and into the tunnel that would take them to Blythe and beyond. Jax and his seatmate made small talk as the maglev hurtled under the valley and mountains to the east.

"Is Chicago your home?" Jax asked.

"No, I'm on business. I travel all over the planet. My home is in London. From Chicago, I'll be going there for two weeks R&R."

As they burst out of the tunnel into full sunlight, Jax was dazzled by the gently rolling dried-out scrub ground and occasional Joshua tree cactus.

"Look. There to the southeast, you can see the first of the gantries and towers that make up the spaceport."

Within moments the train was surrounded by the towering machines and support gantries that covered the 2,200 square-mile complex. There was a bustle in the carriage as people began to collect their belongings in anticipation of arrival.

"Here. You're going to the moon and you might find this interesting."

The man handed Jax a copy of the Luna City News, the Lunatics local print and e-zine publication.

"Thanks, don't you need this for your trip to Chicago?"

"Nah, I read it this morning. It was just stuck in my case. You'll get more use from it than me. Enjoy."

The maglev was pulling into the transport center and, as the doors aligned, passengers began to move about. Once stopped, those departing moved to and through the doors and onto the platform.

Jax wished his seatmate a great trip and exited the maglev.

On the transit board, he saw the 15:00 shuttle was scheduled to depart on time and that meant he had just over three hours before he could board. He headed toward the shops and restaurants that surrounded the area and selected one that had a dark interior and soft music.

He sat at the bar and ordered a beer. There was no one to his right and, to his left, a man about five years younger than he. The stemmed glass sitting in front of him on the bar held the remnants of a dirty martini and an olive.

"Going up or down?" he asked.

He was good-looking with sandy blonde hair, sparkling blue eyes, and a compact physic.

"Up," Jax replied. Then added,

"I'm on the 15:00 shuttle to Delhi 2 and from there to the moon. What about you?"

"I'm on the 16:00 shuttle to Delhi 1, then on to Titan."

"Seems we have enough time for a drink or two and something to eat. Have you had lunch, yet?"

"No, but maybe you'd like to join me for a bite?"

"I was thinking the same thing."

They ordered a second round of drinks and then a small meal. Afterward, they continued to chat and the man, whose name was David, asked,

"Why don't we get a capsule for an hour or two?"

Jax had already thought the same thing and was ready with an answer.

"Sure," he said. "But I can't stay too long."

"Sounds good to me."

They paid the bill, found the capsule hotel, and spent the next hour and a half with one another. Jax then made his way to the launch shuttle and what he hoped would be a non-eventful trip.

As he entered the passenger waiting room, he saw Charlemagne Beckman standing at a coffee bar on the other side of the area . There was no way for Jax to avoid an encounter so he crossed the space and stood next to Chuck.

"I thought you were on the early shuttle. What happened?"

Surprised, Chuck turned to look at Jax and let out a chuckle.

"Well, I was hoping to see you before boost. The 9:00 shuttle was canceled for passengers. They moved all of us to later shuttles and I just happened to be assigned this one."

Jax didn't believe Chuck was assigned to this shuttle by accident and assumed he had used his connections to get onboard with Jax.

"What a surprise," Jax said, then added,

"I'll bet you also happen to be seated next to me. Right?"

"Oh, I don't know. What level are you on?"

"Level 4, seat 16A."

"Now, this really is a bit of good luck. I'm on Level 4, seat 16B. So, yes, I'm seated next to you. We can continue our discussion from last night."

"Are you by chance also on the later shuttle I'm on to the moon?" Jax asked with a touch of sarcasm.

"Sorry, I wish it were so, but I have meetings until tomorrow afternoon. I'll catch the shuttle after that. Still, we have a few more minutes to talk about the moon."

Jax and Chuck took the transport out to the launch pad where the shuttle to Delhi 2 was in preparation for departure. They walked through the passenger lounge and toward the shuttle. Once outside they stood to look at the ship that would shortly rocket them to the heavens.

"It doesn't look that large."

"It's large enough to boost us into space. It can only carry two hundred passengers or the equivalent in freight. Today's manifest is a mix of passengers, 61, and the remainder freight. Do you see anyone else from LMC that will be boarding?"

"I don't. Jax lied. He knew almost half his team would be on board with the rest already on Delhi 2 waiting for the 18:30 shuttle to the moon. But he didn't know Chuck well enough to fully trust him. As he climbed the steps to the airlock, he noticed he was surrounded by many business people on their way to the space platform and from there either the moon or one of the planets. They entered the vessel and were in the small reception area from which ladders to the upper and lower levels led passengers to their assigned seats.

"This way," Chuck said and headed up the small ladder to level 4. As they ascended, he continued.

"The only description for these shuttles is Spartan. Dull grey and unadorned. Nothing extra at all. It's the cost to escape Earth's gravity well that requires a huge amount of resources to boost each kilogram into orbit. It all costs money and the payloads have to compensate for the expense."

They stepped onto level 4 and Chuck, once again, led the way to their seats.

"Your gravcouch is there and mine's here. Take a seat and the screen will light up for you. Then, just use the touch pad on the right arm to adjust right, left, up, and down."

As Jax sat down the screen came to life and he was rewarded with a magnificent view out over the spaceport facing north. He was excited to be able to watch their departure and was looking forward to the experience of leaving the Earth for the second time. Jax was fastening his restraints when the flight droid came over and stood between him and the screen.

"Welcome, sir, to flight # 1128 to space platform Delhi 2. May I scan your travel voucher?"

Jax took his comm out and opened the voucher page which the droid quickly scanned with a pad located on the inside of his forearm.

"You are booked for this flight and will transfer to lunar shuttle flight # 226 which departs Delhi 2 at 18:30. Do you require any assistance?" the droid asked.

"No, thank you" Jax replied.

The droid moved on to Chuck and the other passengers as three more stepped off the ladder and took their seats. There was now a light buzz of conversation in the cabin and most of the passengers for this level had arrived and were settling in for the 90-minute flight to Delhi 2. As he sat looking over the landscape a shuttle lifted off at the far side of the port and left an exhaust trail in the sky as it pushed toward space.

"We'll climb out toward the southeast as we lift toward orbit and you'll be able to see everything on your viewscreen."

He was watching a crew prepare a shuttle close to his when the seat slowly started to rotate back and stretch out flat. He also saw set into the ceiling another view screen which was showing the same view as the screen he had just been watching. He wasn't tense so much as excited as he awaited what would come next.

"This is the captain. In preparation for liftoff all passengers should be in their assigned seats, restraints fastened and couches reclined. Flight droids to stasis positions, crew to liftoff positions. T-minus 60 seconds to initial boost. Captain out."

Jax was still working on the screen controls when he discovered he could access the view from the cockpit. At the moment all it showed was a clear sky but Jax knew when they closed in on Delhi 2 the view would be very different.

As he switched the view to face south again, he felt a shudder run through the shuttle and heard a low deep rumble as the powerful engines engaged and began to push the ship skyward. Jax watched as the spaceport began to drop away from view and the mountains and far landscapes came into sight. The shuttle's speed was increasing by the moment and Jax was pushed firmly into his gravcouch at four times his usual weight.

"Don't worry," Chuck said. "This will only last about two minutes. After that, the shuttle will throttle back its engines slightly for the first maneuver to place it in an initial low-Earth orbit. From there it will lift to match the geosynchronous orbit of Delhi 2 floating at an altitude of 42,000 meters above the Earth."

With increasing speed, the shuttle passed through fifteen thousand meters and Jax watched as the blue of the sky deepened and all he could see was the far horizon from the viewer. He felt the power drop slightly and as the shuttle began to rotate the receding Earth filled his viewer once again. Moments later the ship passed through thirty thousand meters and Jax could see the western edge of the Gulf of Mexico.

"Keep your eyes on the screen, now. You'll see the western edge of what had been Florida before global warming raised the Earth's seas and much of the coastline became submerged under the rising water levels."

Jax also saw the terminator separating night from day quickly approaching and watched in wonder as the shuttle passed into night high above the Earth. The view below had few lights as they hurtled out over the South Atlantic Ocean toward the African continent. Jax switched over to the view from the cockpit and was rewarded with a spectacular view of a black sky spangled with stars and a rising quarter moon.

Suddenly Jax felt weightless as the engines ceased to fire and the shuttle continued its climb out of the Earth's gravity well.

"We'll circle the Earth two times before reaching the same geosynchronous orbit as the space platform. So how do you feel now that you've experienced two launches into space?"

"Thanks, Chuck. Glad you were along."

The restraints kept him in place and the gravcouch slowly returned to an upright position. With a broad smile on his face, Jax relished the idea that he was on his way to a new life on a distant satellite.

CHAPTER FOUR

Chuck talked almost nonstop since boosting into space and Jax wanted nothing more than to arrive at the platform. Then, through the forward viewscreen, Jax saw it. Delhi 2. He interrupted Chuck to point at the screen.

"I don't know why, but I thought we would see a wheel spinning in space."

"Ever since inertial suppression systems came into being with the advent of transluminal travel, everything in space is a platform. Delhi 1 was built as a wheel but later transformed into a platform. Gravity is maintained at 80% Earth normal."

Jax was amazed at the sheer size of the platform. It was a very large collection of docking facilities spreading in all directions with housing for residents and tourists, dry docks, and warehouses for the efficient movement of cargo to and from the Earth's surface.

"There are so many ships surrounding the platform. The larger ones must be transluminal transports, but what are the intermediate sizes used for"

"Those are lunar shuttles. I know they don't look very efficient, but they get the job done. Look, we're about to enter our mooring."

The shuttle slowed and was entering the designated arrivals bay. As Jax watched, the space platform seemed to envelop the craft as it settled to the decking. Within moments gravity was restored as the shuttle became part of the platform by touching down. A large umbilicus moved toward the airlock of the shuttle and quickly connected it to the arrivals hall. Jax felt the slight change of pressure as the airlock was opened to allow access to the platform.

"This is the captain. Please make your way to the airlock and from there the arrivals hall where you will be directed to your ongoing flights. As a reminder, the gravity maintained on this platform is 80% that of Earth and you may find slight disorientation as you stand and begin to move about the cabin. Safe travels and welcome to Delhi 2. Captain out."

"No need to rush, Jax. Why don't you wait a minute while these other passengers get their space legs?"

"I'll also have to get my space legs. If you don't mind, Chuck, I'm going to join the others. I hope your meetings go as planned. See you on the moon."

He could feel the slight difference in gravity and took his first tentative steps toward the ladder and the airlock below. He very quickly got the hang of moving about and within minutes was crossing the umbilicus to arrivals where he passed his comm over a scanner to move through the area and out to the main concourse. There he found shops and restaurants for those passengers not staying on Delhi 2 for any length of time. He found a small bar off the main corridor which looked cozy and quiet. As he entered, a service droid showed him to a small table set away from the entrance.

"How may I serve you today, sir?" the droid asked.

"I'll have a Cerillion brandy and a menu," Jax said as he surveyed the room, and the droid left to get the order. There were only three other customers in the bar and a small droid band played a soft blend of galactic jazz in one corner of the space.

The droid arrived with his drink and menu and Jax motioned him to stay.

"Wait a moment and I'll give you my order," Jax said as he began to peruse the items on the menu. He quickly found his favorite synth-steak which would be served with a tofu baked potato and a small salad and told the droid to bring another brandy when he brought the food. Jax knew the food was synthetic or hydroponically grown but the tastes were as close to real as possible. In space, there wasn't room for live animals to supply the needs of the millions of people who now populated the Orion arm of the Milky Way galaxy. He was enjoying the music when he felt a touch on his shoulder and saw a shadow fall across the table. He turned to see a nondescript man in an outdated and worn platform jumpsuit smiling and taking the seat across from Jax.

"Hello, I'm a friend of Charlemagne Breckman and he told me this morning to look you up while you were on Delhi 2. I'm sorry I didn't meet you as you left the shuttle. Chuck thought you might be interested in a little more history of the Moon and Luna City."

"You boys just don't give up, do you? You must also go to the same garb shop," Jax laughed, "you both dress a lot alike."

"Chuck is my brother and yes, I guess we both do have a slightly dated sense of style. My name is John Breckman and Chuck believes you might not have all the facts of what's going on at Luna City and the new Aitken Base."

"He and I did talk a bit about the crowding that's going on and how it might affect future operations," Jax said.

"You don't understand what's been happening over the past ten years on the moon and the other mining facilities around the solar system. More than four thousand people have died working in the mines and LMC continues to ignore the most basic safety regulations in its unbridled quest for profits. At the same time, they make it impossible for any of the miners to leave once they get to a specific mine. The wages are so low and the cost of everything they need so high no one can save enough to buy transportation back to Earth. There is seething unrest throughout the system and it's only a matter of time before the miners and citizens are forced to take action against the LMC."

Jax's food and second drink arrived and the droid placed them in front of him.

"Would you like something, sir?" the droid asked John.

"I'll also have a Cerillion brandy."

The droidtender turned and went for the drink.

"Hold it, John. LMC would send additional men and women to protect its assets. Also, not everyone on the moon works for the mines."

"Chuck believes the civilian population will join the miners in any action they take and I believe we are looking at a final confrontation between the LMC forces on the moon and other planets and satellites if things don't change," John said.

"You're taking a job as assistant to the command of all infrastructures on the moon and you need to know the facts. Chuck and I maintain connections between all the mines throughout the system and all of us will ultimately decide what needs to be done to bring LMC under control. Chuck feels you're the right man to help us work with LMC to bring some sort of justice to the way things are run. He also believes you will be discrete about the conversations we are having at the moment."

John's drink arrived and the droid left them alone.

"I don't know enough, yet, to make any kind of assurance as to my actions on the moon. I will, however, keep your thoughts to myself until I can reach some sort of decision if I need to." Jax said.

John threw his brandy back with one swift motion and stood up facing Jax.

"There's trouble coming and Chuck wants you to be prepared. He also wants you to know he'll work with you if he can. Ultimately the lunar government and the population will take control of not only the mines but the whole moon. From there the same actions will spread out to the other planets and moons in the solar system. The small security forces in place will be inadequate when the moment comes. At some point, you will be forced to choose sides and Chuck hopes you'll be able to work with him before the inevitable happens. Safe travels." John said as he walked away.

Jax could only stare at the retreating figure. What was he getting himself into?

CHAPTER FIVE

Jax was in the departure lounge awaiting his 18:30 flight and looking out the viewport at the ship that would carry him to the moon. The transport, *Over the Moon*, would have a passenger load of 162, a crew of 8, and numerous service droids to take care of the needs of the passengers as well as steveadroids working the freight decks.

The surrounding passengers were pointing at the ship and talking about their upcoming journey.

"*Over the Moon* is a large vessel," a man was telling his son. "She's 478 meters in length and has a beam of 68 meters. Just over 75% of the vessel is fuel cells and propulsion."

"Will we be going faster than the speed of light?"

"The ship is equipped with the latest inertial suppression system but is not capable of superluminal flight. The boost out of orbit will be over 8 gees until she reaches cruising speed then we'll just coast to the moon and Tycho Base. The engines will stop us when we get close enough."

The umbilicus doors opened and the passengers began to make their way toward the transport. As Jax stepped through the large airlock into reception he was amazed at the size of the area and the luxurious look of the finishes and furnishings.

"Welcome aboard *Over the Moon*, sir. May I scan your comm for ticket and passage information?" the stewardroid asked. Jax passed his comm over the reader set into the inside of the droid's forearm like the other droids he had seen today.

"Suite # 26 forward. Please follow me." As they moved across the reception area it continued.

"Your cabin is in the executive and officer area of the ship just behind the cockpit and close to the recreation facilities as well as the restaurants and bars. *Over the Moon* is also equipped with a large view lounge with vidscreens for port, starboard, forward, and stern views and it will be very popular as we get closer to the moon."

The ship was luxurious compared to the shuttle he had just departed and Jax continued to be amazed at the size of the transport and the beauty of the interiors. He and the droid were in the cabin area and from time to time they would pass an open door to an interior where Jax would see handsome people beginning to settle in for the crossing. He had evening clothes to change into once he reached his cabin and would be able to enjoy the ship as just another passenger.

"Cabin # 26, sir. Please place your palm on the plaque to the right of the door. This will imprint your palm and no one else will be able to access your cabin except the stewardroid."

Jax did as instructed and the door slid away with a quiet hiss. The suite was spacious by transport standards with a large bed, nightstands, and small dresser along with a desk and comm screen. The head contained a full shower and dryer station as well as the other usual amenities. There was also a small sofa set across from a wall with a vidscreen showing the Delhi 2 landing bay at the moment. The droid explained the amenities of the suite and within moments Jax was left alone to contemplate his next move. His luggage had already been delivered and unpacked so all he had to do was select what to wear and start exploring the ship.

"This is the captain. All crew prepare for departure. Droids to stasis. Will all passengers please be aware there might be a slight sense of disorientation as we maneuver out of our landing bay and into our position for departure. Once there we'll torch the engines and boost for the moon. Departure will be in one minute. Captain out."

Jax looked in the closet and selected a pale pink shirt, navy blue trousers, and a fawn-colored jacket that would be comfortable as well as dressy enough for dinner later that evening. He would be able to take a look around, have a drink, and reach the dining room in plenty of time for his first meal in space.

There was no indication or sense of movement as the transport departed Delhi 2. It was only after Jax finished dressing that he noticed his vidscreen was now showing a black void studded with stars. He left his cabin and headed aft in search of the various lounges and recreational areas the droid had mentioned. He exited the cabin corridor and walked into a large atrium area surrounded by all the ship had to offer. He found the view lounge, which was almost full at the moment with passengers trying to get a look at Delhi 2 as the ship departed, and Jax decided not to stay. He shortly found a dark recessed lounge that appealed to him. He entered and found a seat at the bar. The service droid had just come back into service and Jax ordered a Jovan Beer. He looked around the bar and noticed several men and women, all in the uniform of the LMC Management Forces, sitting together. He decided not to announce himself as he had been instructed not to mingle until reaching the moon. His beer arrived just as a single passenger sat one seat away from him and ordered the same thing. After the beer arrived, he turned to Jax and raised his glass, and tilted his head his way as a toast, of sorts.

He was a very handsome man with gorgeous blonde hair, green

eyes, a sturdy build, and a bright inviting smile. Jax returned the gesture and looked away.

"Do you cross often?"

Jax turned back to the man and answered,

"This is my first time and I'm finding it all very exciting. I'm looking forward to our time aboard. How about you?"

"I cross about once a month. I'm stationed on Luna but have business on the Earth which requires my corpus presence. Will you be returning to Earth soon?"

"No, I've taken a job stationed at the new base at Aitken. I'll only be at Tycho base overnight and I don't know the lay of the land there."

"Too bad it's just overnight, there are many things to do at Tycho and, of course, Luna City. I actually enjoy my time on the moon because of the many ways there are to relax and enjoy oneself."

"Maybe once I'm settled in the job, I'll have time off to explore Luna City. But for now, I'll just be passing through. Are you waiting for someone?"

"Oh, my, no. These business trips are never anything but that for me. I usually have my meals alone and spend a lot of time in the view lounge. Are you traveling with anyone?"

"No. I'm on business and my duties don't start until we arrive on the moon. Would you like to join me for dinner?"

"How nice. Yes, I would. Shall we have one more, my treat, before we go to the dining room?"

"Sure," Jax said as he motioned toward the service droid. His presence took his mind off the exchanges he'd had between the Beckman brothers and he suddenly felt transported to a comfortable and inviting place. He felt so uplifted he ordered dirty gin martinis for the two of them and thought about where the evening might lead. As exciting as his first transit to the moon might be, the thought of hopefully spending time with this striking man would make the adventure that much more exhilarating.

"My name is Martin Kauri and I'm employed by the Lunar Management Company in the procurement and asset protection department."

Jax was impressed and this tidbit raised his opinion of him even higher than it already was. He, however, was more taken by his appearance as they walked from the bar to the dining room. He was 5'8" of a tall well-built man with striking blonde hair cut short, emerald green eyes, and an inviting smile. His movements were assured as they walked and Jax enjoyed having him on his arm in what, for him, was a very courtly gesture and not at all his usual style.

"I'm Jason Escobar and also work for LMC. We'll have a lot to talk about, I'm sure." He said as they headed for the dining room.

They dined and took a walk after dinner to enjoy the view lounge and have a little more time to get to know one another.

"I've met people all over the Earth on my travels but being on a ship headed for the moon makes the whole thing somehow more compressed and exciting," Jax said. They were sitting in a small alcove off the main reception area and Jax wanted to get closer.

"It's been a long day and I'm ready for a little shuteye. I'm down this corridor." Martin said.

Jax walked with him to his stateroom and, with a light kiss, Martin invited him in. They slept late and enjoyed breakfast in a sparsely filled dining room. By the end of the day, they were almost inseparable. After dinner on the second night, Jax and Martin were once again in the view lounge, and as predicted by the steward droid the room was full of passengers enjoying the view.

"Look at them, Martin. You'd think they had never seen the moon before." Jax said.

Martin turned to him and said,

"They should be excited. The view is so different up here. The moon from the arth, seen through 120 Kilometers of atmosphere, is a softly diffused orb with smooth transitions between the shadows of the volcanic mountains and the bright reflectiveness of the impressive impact craters. From space, and at this distance of only 90,000 kilometers, the moon becomes a large and spectacularly defined space satellite. Only this close can you see the details so brutally defined by solar radiation, meteorite impacts, and the brightness of the sun."

"I know we've started braking for arrival but it still seems as if we're floating in space with no movement," Jax said.

"Here we are suspended in the void. I almost wish we could stay here forever." Martin said as he snuggled close to Jax. They talked of this and that and finally the crush of people began to thin out. It was 00:30 hours and they were alone surrounded by the magnificent view of the approaching satellite. The space was brightly lit by the sunlight reflected off the moon's surface and Jax could see every detail of Martin's beautiful face. He leaned to him and kissed him softly on the cheek. Martin turned to Jax and returned the kiss on his lips. They held each other that way for a moment then slowly separated.

"You know I can't get you out of my mind right now, don't you? I suppose you'll say it's simply a shipboard romance." He said as they looked at one another.

"It's more than that for me, Martin. I don't know the full details of my new job but I'll get leave every time you're working on the moon. I'll come to Luna City and we can be together. Is that alright with you?"

There's something you need to know about me and my job on the moon. Procurement of supplies is my primary function and I take my work very seriously; but, I'm also in contact with a group that would like to negotiate with the LMC, and in particular, Joseph Warren and Reginald Tebaldi. I believe the group has a valid point about safety in the mines throughout the solar system and the appallingly horrific working conditions at all locations. I know your position with LMC is municipal management and I don't want you to think I'm trying to use you in any way. Get settled in your new job and get the lay of the land at Aitken outpost and on the moon in general. The next time I come back we'll have a chance to talk about what you will see and what you will learn."

"You're the third person in as many days to warn me about the LMC and the conditions throughout the system. My research didn't reveal anything like the information each of you has told me. I've also been getting conflicting orders from the very people you seem to know so well. It all just doesn't add up for me."

"Let me give you a little history lesson. The moon was just a rock until the colonist decided to take control of its future. In 2089 they created the Lunar Compact which put control of the satellite in the hands of its citizens for the first time. By 2127 the lunatics, as they like to call themselves, achieved self-sufficiency and became an independent entity. Now there are over 95,000 citizens of the moon mostly based in and around Tycho Base. Luna City was sold off by LMC in 2279 when it opened Tycho Base and the center of activity moved there. The public dome is bright and airy and the shops and restaurants are great. Luna City became The Pleasure Zone and is owned almost entirely by Lunatics."

"What kind of reaction did you get from LMC? Do they care?""They say they don't, but there is a concerted effort by LMC to crush any talk of independence from the Earth."

"Whoa, independence? How would the moon survive without supplies and the constant freight and passenger travel?"

"This little satellite is far more valuable than most people realize. Its strategic position close to the Earth and its unlimited ability to send ships out into the cosmos far more easily than lifting everything directly from the planet."

"I know the nanorobots create the domes, housing, solar farms, water, and oxygen for everyone but LMC still has a large presence and won't like the Lunatics deciding when and how mining will be done on the moon."

"At some point, they will have no choice. The lunatics will eventually take control of their own home. LMC won't be able to stop it."

"Lunatics already own more than 80% of Tycho Base City and they are about to rename it New Luna City. LMC won't be able to do as they please for much longer. That, my dear Jason, is the moon you are about to set foot on for the first time."

Martin looked directly into Jason's eyes. There was tenderness there and something else Jason couldn't read. He returned the gentle stare and then kissed him slowly and deeply. They parted from one another and Martin said,

"Relax. You won't be able to figure it all out until you start working on the job. Then you'll have more access to information and be able to see the conditions for yourself. Until then, let's enjoy the view. We'll be landing in about 8 hours and I don't want to miss a moment with you."

CHAPTER SIX

Moose Nkosi was seated at his desk in the Tycho Base offices looking over the list of new security officers arriving on this morning's shuttle from Earth. Among them was his new sixth in command, Jason Escobar, who he had been informed was now his second in command at Aitken Base. He met Jason, via vid hookup with the Earth offices of the Lunar Management Company, during the interview process and hadn't formed any kind of opinion as to how Jason would fit in with the team already in place. Along with Jason, another thirty lower-level officers, most of whom assumed they would be serving at Tycho Base, were arriving. It would be Nkosi's task to explain their new duties at the mine at Aitken basin. Nkosi had already made sure the outpost there was prepared for the influx of new officers as they would be in Tycho only overnight before shipping to Aitken.

"Tina, come in, please," Moose said into the app on his desk.

His assistant, Tina Markle, had worked with him since he came to LMC and she knew him inside out.

"Yes, boss. Before you start, I'll fill you in. Walters is already on his way over to the transit center. He has the list and will take them to quarters once they've completed arrival procedures."

"Good. The changes sent from Reginald Tebaldi and by extension, Joseph Warren, worry me. They aren't going to be happy going out to Aitken Base so soon after arriving. What more can you tell me about

Escobar? I met once on-screen during the interview process. You've read his file and processed his digital resume. Is there anything I should know?"

"You know everything I know, boss. He'll be a good addition and he should be able to keep his crew in check if we have any trouble."

"Fine. Thanks. Let me know when they arrive. I'll go over to meet them."

Tina left and Moose stared at the closed door. Then, he thought about how he had gotten here and how he had changed. He spent the last seven years working for LMC and Joseph Warren. It was there he met Reginald Tebaldi and from him discovered the dark underside of city, outpost, and mine management. As he discovered, it was always about the money, not the citizens and employees. Through manipulation, both overt and covert, Tebaldi slowly made Nkosi his pawn and his maneuvers involved him in decisions and protocols that ultimately endangered every citizen of the solar system. Along with it, he was able to make it appear the decisions were Nkosi's alone and now, through blackmail, was his to use as he saw fit. Every order came from him and he knew those orders were ultimately from Joseph Warren.

The Lunar Management Company, with Warren making most of the decisions, also controlled the cost of everything from oxygen to water, food to clothing, and medical care to unemployment and made sure the miners and citizens barely made enough to survive. Once placed on a planet or moon, there was no way to save enough from wages to ever travel back to Earth. He knew it was wrong not to allow these people a choice of when and how they chose to work. But, he had been forced into a corner by Tebaldi and knew there was nothing he could do to change their plight.Moose looked up as his secretary came into his office.

"You better get a move on, boss. The shuttle arrives within ten minutes and you said you wanted to meet this one."

"Thanks. I'm just leaving."

As he walked, he thought about the new arrivals. He would try to make their first few hours on the moon as easy as possible. What he was going to have to tell them in the morning was not going to be pleasant. Reginald's instructions had been explicit and he couldn't make changes to what he had been told. Then, his mind wandered to his past and what his life had been.

Musawenkosi Nkosi was born in the Republic of South Africa in 2269 on the decimated continent of Africa. The Ebola outbreak of 2071 – 2075 killed more than 1.4 billion people and the continent became a wasteland with fewer than forty million people spread thinly throughout the landmass. Both his parents were killed when he was four in a short-lived turf war between rival gangs located in and around Johannesburg. He survived by chance because he had been playing outside his home behind a small garden shed. The roving gangs simply missed him and moved to other houses along his dusty little street. When he became hungry and walked back to the house, he discovered his parents on the floor in the front room of their small run-down bungalow. When he couldn't get them to move, he ran from his house yelling for help from anyone. Many of the families in the neighborhood had been victims of the same attack and at first, Musawenkosi was unable to find anyone to help. Eventually, a small squad of proctors arrived and began to sort out the carnage and help the survivors. Musawenkosi had run back to his house when the proctors arrived and it was there he was found with a pistol in his hand protecting his parent's bodies.

"All right, kid, we're not going to hurt you. We're on your side. What happened here?" the leader of the small squad asked.

"I don't know. Don't come closer. I want my Mama." Musawenkosi said

"They're dead, kid. Do you have any family in the area? Do you go to school?" The proctor asked.

"Papa and Mama are the only ones I know. Don't come any closer."

"Put the gun down. You'll have to come with us."

Musawenkosi stood in one spot for a moment and tears started falling down his cheeks and the gun slipped from his hand. He turned left and right then twirled around and started to run out the back of the house but was stopped by a proctor standing in the kitchen. The man grabbed at Musawenkosi but the child twisted out of his grasp. He was still going toward the back door when a second, much taller proctor, tackled him and pulled him to the floor.

"Easy, easy, we're not going to hurt you. Calm down." the proctor said.

As Musawenkosi began to calm down and his breathing became more regular the man lessened his grip and helped the child stand up.

"There. You'll feel better in a minute. What's your name?"

"Moose."

"Moose? What's your real name?"

"Musawenkosi Nkosi." He replied.

"Well, Moose, you're going to have to come along with me to my headquarters. My name is Langa Gazini and I'll make sure no one hurts you. Okay?" Gazini smiled as he spoke softly to Musawenkosi and the boy slowly raised his eyes to the man's face and said,

"Uh, huh. Gosh, you're tall."

Gazini laughed and pulled the boy closer to him.

"You'll be fine, kid. Come on, let's get out of here."

Gazini took the boy out the back door and around to the waiting squad cars.

He placed Musawenkosi in the back seat and closed the door. There were no handles in the back seats and a plasteel screen between the front and back. At first, Musawenkosi was nervous, but Gazini immediately calmed him down.

"Hey, most kids your age would be glad to go cruising around in a proctor car. I'll be sitting right here in front. This is Jackson, and he'll be driving us to the station. Sit back and enjoy the ride," Gazini said as he turned to face front and the car slowly pulled away from the house Musawenkosi would never see again.

Langa Gazini had been married for twelve years and his wife worked as a nurse in the only large hospital in Johannesburg. They had no children and both were seemingly comfortable with the arrangement. Between his work and his home life, Langa seemed a very happy and satisfied man. Langa took Musawenkosi to the headquarters and turned him over to a woman who specialized in childhood trauma. He went to his office and started the paperwork explaining the gang incident he had just come from. His mind kept going back to Musawenkosi Nkosi and how fierce he appeared with the gun in his hand standing over his dead parents. The boy had courage even if he didn't yet know it. Langa smiled with the thought that kept coming to his mind. Why not, he wondered. Why not? He quickly finished his paperwork and went to look for the boy he now called Moose.

Through the glass wall surrounding the office, he could see Moose was still with the social worker but it looked as if they were almost finished. He knocked softly on the door and opened it.

"Is everything alright in here? How're you doing, Moose? Is she treating you okay?"

"I'm okay, Mr. Gazini, but I'm a little tired, I guess."

35

"Whata' you say, doc. Is he okay to leave?"

"He's fine. I wish there were a family member we could contact but the only place for him right now is the protective services dormitory," she said in a subdued voice.

"Doc, I've got an idea. Why don't I take him home with me? My wife and I have plenty of room and I'm sure he needs people around over the next week or two who will help him come to terms with what happened." Gazini suggested.

"Let me talk to my boss, but I think it's a great idea. What do you think, Musawenkosi?" she said in a bright and happy voice. She didn't wait for a reply but left the room in search of her immediate superior.

"I'm okay with that, I guess," he said in a quiet voice as he turned to Langa. "Will I stay with you for a long time?"

"We'll see about that, but for the moment don't worry about having to leave. You'll be safe with us and we'll help you find out what to do next." Langa said.

Musawenkosi, who became known far and wide as Moose, remained with Langa Gazini and his wife until he graduated from college with a degree in Law Enforcement and Municipal Management. Moose had grown as tall as Langa and was a strong man with a sense of fair play and justice. His ebony skin, black hair, and deep brown eyes made him attractive and popular with his friends. Langa and Moose became more father and son than many of the other kids he knew. After college, Gazini helped Moose get a job in New Manhattan in the America's Alliance with a division of the Lunar Management Company. Called the Urban Management Division, it oversaw the efficient operations of cities all over the globe and the solar system. When the day came for Moose to board the suborbital flight to New Manhattan, he hugged Langa and said,

"When you found me I was frightened and didn't know what would happen to me or where I would go. You've given me a chance at life I might never have known. I love you for that. I'll come back when I have learned what it is I truly want."

"No, don't come back. There's nothing for you here. The planets and stars are where you belong. I knew the first day I saw you standing over your parent's bodies with a gun in your hand you had the courage it takes to become a fine man. We love you and hope you will find success and happiness wherever you go from here."

They embraced one last time and Moose walked toward the departure gate. There, alone, he did something he hadn't done since he was four years old. He cried.

CHAPTER SEVEN

Over the Moon slowed to three meters a second and was quickly coming into range of Tycho Base and Luna City. The shuttle was 100 meters above the moon's regolith and continued to slow as control brought her in. They were passing over the elevated impact crater rim formed by the ejecta from the collision. Jax and Martin were in the observation lounge watching as the ship was carefully slowed even more as the base came into complete view.

"Every time I come here, I think it looks so barren," Martin said, "and if I didn't know better, I would think we had landed at the wrong place. Still, I do enjoy being here and you've helped make the trip so much more interesting than usual. We'll touchdown in about four minutes."

Tycho Base was an amazing complex of large landing pads with access buildings and storage warehouses around each one.

"Look over there," Martin said. You can see the solar farm which supplies Luna City and Tycho Base with the electricity needed to survive," Martin explained.

"The electricity from the farm also powers the oxygen manufacturing system as well as the hydroponics farms and water filtration systems."

"As large and imposing as all this is I'm amazed that the majority of the infrastructure on this and all bases and mines on moons and planets around the system is underground. I know that protects the inhabitants from the vicious radiation emanating from the sun and flowing throughout the system, but do the inhabitants find it uncomfortable sometimes?"

"Everyone has learned to adjust. The new dome at Tycho Base is expansive and full of light. Citizens come together there and for most, it alleviates the sense of claustrophobia. There's also the added benefit of helping to maintain an ambient temperature in the warrens suitable for human life. And being underground helps maintain constant pressure and oxygen content as well as protect the structures from almost all meteorites and other debris that might fall to the moon's surface," Martin added.

Jax and Martin watched as *Over the Moon* slipped across the threshold of the landing pad and began to make a 90-degree turn in place which would line up the airlock with the umbilicus already making its way out to the ship. He was momentarily disoriented as the ship touched the lunar surface, the inertial suppression system was disengaged and everyone on board suddenly weighed only 16% of their Earth weight. The one thing that hadn't changed, however, was the amount of mass each one carried and people were already pushing too hard or trying to stop too quickly which was causing small pileups at entryways and passageways.

"This happens every time I come Lunaside. The untrained flail around and it takes them a long time to adjust. The droids will help, but many of these people will never get the hang of glide-walking on the moon. Let's wait here for a few minutes before we disembark. Okay?"

"Fine with me," Jax said with a smile. "I just have to report to my new base commander once I've disembarked. Where will you go after we disembark?"

"I'm staying at the Luna Metropole over in Luna City. It helps me to get away from the office while I'm here and gives me a chance to meet with locals and hear all the gossip as well as the hard facts of what's going on."

"Look, Martin, I won't question your intentions but would remind you the LMC still holds the power to send people home or end their employment. Just don't do anything rash. Okay?"

For a moment Jax thought he might not answer. The look in his eyes was opaque and disclosed nothing. Then, just as suddenly, his face unfolded into a broad smile.

"Don't worry, Jax, I have no intention of placing myself in jeopardy at this time. I'll finish my work and meet with a few of the people who'll let me know what we need to do next. I'm not starting a revolution tomorrow, I promise."

"I'll comm you once I reach Aitken Base and get settled in. Is that alright?"

"Fine, Jax, but neither one of us will have a lot of time to chat over the next few days. It's time we started moving toward the airlock. Look, most of the other passengers have left or finally gotten the hang of lunar gliding."

Jax was trained before he left Earth on the subtle glide/walk most Lunatics used once they grew accustomed to and comfortable with the lighter gravity. He and Martin easily made their way to the airlock and into the umbilicus toward the reception area.

"Okay, this is it. You made this crossing memorable for me in so many ways and I'll be in touch as soon as I'm settled at Aitken. By the way, you know I want to see you again, don't you?"

"Jax, you old softy. Of course we'll see more of each other. I'll wait for your message. For now, bye."

Martin touched his cheek, turned, and made his way to immigration and customs. Jax watched him walk away with a short pang in his heart. Okay, buddy boy, time to focus on meeting Nkosi and the rest of your new team. The LMC management team had a separate processing area and Jax saw there were at least thirty men and women standing and waiting to be cleared. A man was holding a sign with numerous names and Jax saw his as he got closer.

"Jason Escobar, reporting for duty."

"Step over there Mr. Escobar, and wait until your name is called. Have your comm ready with your orders and immigration papers."

Jax did as he was told and joined the group he had seen as he left Martin's side. He was closer to the group now and thought they weren't a bad-looking bunch of men and women. Each seemed to be comfortable moving about in the new lighter gravity and Jax gently put his bag on the floor and stood to await his turn.

"You handled that nicely, I see. You certainly benefitted from the training on Earth to prepare you for this gravity and the moon," a woman to his left said with a small smile on her face.

"Yeh, training helped. Having an idea of where things are going to be also helped. I knew, for instance, we would all be meeting in this part of the reception area." Jax answered back and returned the smile.

"For a recruit, you're better informed than me, that's for sure. They just put me on board, gave me the necessary papers, and wished me a safe trip. Thirty-six hours later and here I am talking to another recruit. I'm Amanda Flannigan, Andie to my friends. What's your job description, soldier?"

"None of us are soldiers, we're management officers for the LMC, and I'm Jason Escobar your new commanding officer. Welcome to the moon."

41

"Sir, I'm sorry sir, I didn't have any idea, sir. I'm sorry, sir. I wouldn't have ...."

"Can it, Flannigan, no harm done and it's great to begin to meet some of my team," Jason added another smile and turned to watch the remaining team members arrive in the reception area.

Jason was called to the front and he walked away from the vocal recruit. Her idea of what they were and how they were going to operate on the moon gave him just a tic of concern. If all the recruits were under the assumption they were "soldiers" then the LMC was creating something different from what he had signed up to lead.

"Scan here, sir, and turn to your right. Keep your eyes open for a retinal scan. Thank you, sir, step to your right through that door. Next!"

Jax walked through the designated door and saw a tall and imposing man in an LMC Security uniform standing near a small group of similarly dressed men and women.

"Escobar, I'm Commander Musawenkosi Nkosi and you'll be reporting directly to me. These are a few of your new officers. I'll let each of them make introductions once we get you over to headquarters. I believe you understand from your orders all of these men and women will be accompanying you to Aitken tomorrow morning to assume the duties of security and safety. Welcome to the moon."

So, Jax thought, what happened to municipal management and the job I was hired to do? Charles Breckman, his brother, and then Martin had each, in their way, tried to prepare Jax for this moment and he was looking forward to seeing what happened next.

Nkosi turned and faced the next recruit coming through the door and continued until all the team was assembled and his assistant, Walters, brought the last team member in.

"Walters, here, will show you to the magtube and we'll both be interested to see how you handle yourself in this new gravity. My one suggestion is to get on with it and remember what you were taught on Earth and make it work for you here. Until then, relax today and learn how to move about comfortably. You will have this afternoon and evening for leisure and I'll join you for a short meeting at 21:00 in the officer's meeting compartment. Take 'em away, Walters."

"Follow me and don't fall behind. We're heading over to Tycho Base offices where you'll spend the rest of the day."

Jax watched as Nkosi stood behind to inspect each team member as they began the process of learning how to walk all over again. He was still standing there as Jax rounded a corner to bring up the rear of the group as it made its way to the magtube.

CHAPTER EIGHT

Jax, and what he had already begun to think of as his team, walked toward the magtube platform using the new glide/walk each had learned on Earth. It was easier than moving about in a weightless environment and the team seemed to quickly get the hang of it. Every once in a while, Jax would see a head pop up above the rest as a member would flex his muscles in the lighter gravity and show off to the rest of the team. As the magtube arrived they moved as a group to the rear car where the boarding platform tube was already attached to the train. They boarded the magtube and within moments it began the trip to Tycho Center.

"Has anyone on the team been on the moon, before?" Andie called to the group.

Three hands went up and she leaned toward them and said,

"Keep an eye on these three. They've been here before and should have a good idea of how to move about."

There was subdued chatter among the team and then they burst out of the confines of the platform and onto the surface of the moon. Silence descended on the team as most saw for the first time the surface of the moon close up. The interior of the train was awash in reflected light and all at once, it seemed as if everyone had something to say.

"I never thought it would be so bright."

"When do we get our chance to get onto the surface?"

"Look over there, is that a team on the surface?"

"We'll be out there soon."

"That must be Tycho Center. See the dome and low buildings."

"Hold on, we're about to go underground, again."

The maglev dropped below the surface and they soon arrived at the transit center. They disembarked and were led by Walters to the LMC offices.

"There's a list on the comm screen on the wall. You'll see your name and billet number. The rest of the day is for you to get settled and prepare for the work ahead. Welcome to the moon."

Walters left the room and the team started looking for their quarters. Jax was happily surprised to see he was given private quarters with a small office area included. He had already decided not to unpack much as they would be leaving so soon for Aitkens and the new mine. He did want to wash his face and get a better idea of the lay of the land here at Tycho base and Luna City. He stepped out of the fresher just as the entrance comm announced a visitor.

"Open door," he said and there stood Andie Flannigan.

"May I come in sir and take a moment of your time?" she said.

"Come in, Flannigan, and have a seat," Jax said as he motioned to the chair on the opposite side of his desk. He took the other chair and looked at Flannigan who was a tall, 5'10" woman with blonde hair, deep blue eyes, and a beautiful peaches and cream complexion.

"So, what's on your mind, Flannigan?"

"I didn't want to get off on the wrong foot, sir, and to assure you I have the utmost respect for you and the job I know you will do."

"Let's get one thing straight right now, Flannigan. I'm not a tyrant and don't expect my team to bow and scrape to me. I do expect and hope for mutual respect as we all learn to work together. I look forward to your support as my number two and hope you will help me get this

45

team up to speed as quickly as possible."

"I'm your woman, sir. As I said earlier, things happened so fast for my class. They pushed us through training as quickly as they could then each of us was sent to a different mine. I think I'm lucky to have been sent to the moon. Some of my classmates are still traveling to the outer colonies. We missed a lot of the history of the mines and the company but focused on armaments and tactics for crowd control and suppression. It all seemed just too rushed to me. Still, here I am."

"First of all, we aren't staying here at Tycho Base. We've been reassigned to Aitken. The rest of the team doesn't know this, yet, and I'm sure Nkosi will tell us at the meeting this evening. So, for the moment, keep this to yourself. One of the first things I want to do when we get to Aitken is to sort out the team to find out what training each of them had. Is there anyone in your class here?"

"No, sir. Scuttlebutt says my class was trained with some sort of action expected at the mines but no one knows where there might be trouble and that's why each of us went to a different mine."

"Okay, Flannigan. I'm going to take a look around here and go over to Luna City to see what's there. Meet me here at 20:30 before the 21:00 meeting and we'll compare notes. Try to meet a few of the team and give me some recommendations as to the best fit for some of the jobs we'll need to fill at Aitken. Anything else?"

"No, sir. I'll have a conversation with each team member to help me assess the best fit and I'll be back here at 20:30."

"Thanks."

She stood and left his office. Jax was pleased she had come to see him so soon and believed she would make a good second in command. Her description of the training she received dovetailed with the warnings he had been getting since just before leaving Earth and his feeling

46

of unease increased slightly. He didn't think, however, that Flannigan was part of any plot to destroy Luna City or Tycho Base. He grabbed his jacket and headed over to Luna City.

As the largest and oldest colony in the solar system, Luna City had a reputation as one of the best places to work if you weren't employed by Lunar Mines. It was also touted as the best place to play whether you were with the mines or not. Jax headed for the pleasure zone where he knew he would find an assortment of bars, restaurants, sex clubs, and diversions he hoped would surprise and please. As he walked with the crowds under the vast central pressure dome, he was impressed by the diversity of people and styles of dress that were unlike anything he had ever seen on Earth. Now and then he would see a scruffy panhandler but for the most part, people seemed to know where they were going and headed there at a smart clip. He turned a corner and entered a street that would take him beyond the domed central area and into an area that wasn't as crowded with people in a hurry. The people who were on the street here looked more down at heel and were not as interested in what was going on around them. He was headed into the oldest part of Luna City where the passageways became narrower and lower and the buildings had a worn and dilapidated look. The lighting wasn't as bright and there were dark alleys every few hundred yards with random lighted signs for bars and diners. He decided to head back to the central area and had just turned around when he saw down a side alley a large group of men and women outside one of the seedier clubs with a lighted sign that kept sputtering on and off. The noise from the crowd made him stop and watch what was happening. The people were shouting at someone on the other side of the group and Jax was unable to see who was there. Suddenly there was a loud report from in front of the crowd and they all turned and ran in Jax's direction. He quickly stepped out of the alleyway and watched as the crowd surged past him and poured into the larger street. After they passed, Jax looked back down the alley to see two men in LMC uniforms pick up someone from the street and drag him away from where the crowd had been standing. As he stood there a man who had been part of the crowd came back to look as well.

"Him taken, then?" he said to Jax.

"Yeh. They walked the other way with him between the two guards. What happened and why did they knock him out?"

"It was group speak of Lunar Freedom in hash slinger there with leader types for this burg. The slime hackers was ready to pounce and they grab that guy, Larry King. They told us we no can do then bang, haram-scaram all over hell and back. The peoples pushed here and there and slime hackers grab King. All people run for cover in hash slinger then slime hackers grabem King. Then slime hackers shoot bullets even though against laws for can break dome. Again haram-scaram for people and help no more for King."

Jax recognized the man's speech as Moonglish and even though he had a few hours learning the patois it was an ever-changing mélange of words and phrases used by a small group of mine workers. From what he gathered there had been a meeting of Lunar Freedom in the seedy bar down the alley and Larry King had been elected the new representative from this precinct. It was then he was taken into custody by Lunar Management Company security personnel using guns with bullets that scattered the crowd. The people in the meeting tried to help but were overwhelmed by the security team.

"Where will they take him?" Jax asked.

"Them LMC guys switch him to bar-pad. Prob'ly they rammin' jammin' with maybe digit dance but he no come here again. They kick ass to Earth then no see anymore."

The security team had taken King to jail where they might be torturing him by breaking his fingers. After that, they would send him back to Earth with no chance of working for the company again.

"But that's illegal. There has to be a trial of some sort. He didn't even break the law from what you've said."

"You new here Luna, huh? Peoples try stop Slime hackers get hurt or lights out 'cause mines got to keep open. No more human peoples in mine just slaver types to die in bad fall down. Lunar Freedom for all peoples only way. Kickass LMC back to Earth, you see."

The security teams use force or death to stop any open meetings to work for freedom. The mineworkers were like slaves and could be killed at any time in accidents in the mines. They were calling for Lunar Management Company to leave the moon.

The man turned and hurried down the street away from Jax and the alley.

It was getting late and Jax needed to get back to LMC headquarters for his meeting with Flannigan. He wasn't going to tell her about this incident just yet because he needed to know more about her, Nkosi, the rest of his team, and the true state of the situation at Tycho base and Aitken mine. He also wanted to hear what Nkosi would have to say at this evening's meeting.

CHAPTER NINE

Jax had just returned to his quarters when Flannigan was at his door.

"Come on in, Flannigan. Have a seat. Want something to drink?"

"Thank you, sir," she said as she took the same seat from earlier in the day. "Nothing to drink, sir."

Jax sat down and looked at the woman who was his second in command. Along with her good looks, she was deceptively powerfully built. Underneath the dress uniform of jacket and slacks were shoulders and arms he hadn't noticed when they first met. He also suspected her legs underneath the slacks were shapely as well as strong.

"So, what did you find out about our team, Andi…, uh, Flannigan?"

"If you don't mind, sir, I would appreciate it if you call me Andie in private. It makes me feel more a part of your leadership team."

"Andie, it is, and you should call me Jax. Glad that's settled. Now, who do we have on the team that has any experience, at all?"

"Of the thirty that traveled with us on *Over the Moon*, twenty were trained on Earth and have experience in space, as well. Nine have no experience beyond training at the LMC facility and my experience you know."

"Of that group are there two you think might make a leader similar to a squad leader? We need two people who could take control of half the team as we divide it into two groups?"

"Talk to Isabell Rho and Kirk Chan. Both have off-Earth experience and the conversations I had with each make me believe they have the interest of the miners at heart even though they work for the LMC. Each has a sense of duty to the health and wellbeing of everyone they oversee and don't want to have the company ignore the situation here and around the system. Another thing I discovered from each of them is the unrest that seems to be throughout the system with challenging conditions not only in the mines but in the colonies and support facilities surrounding each mine. Both Rho and Chan experienced small examples of resistance on Mars, Titan, and Phobos. People are unsure of what is going to happen or should happen and they are unhappy."

"Good work, Andie, I'll talk to the two of them tomorrow after we reach Aitken Basin. Keep this to yourself for the moment. Now, let's go hear what Nkosi has to say."

They left for the meeting at the mess and arrived about five minutes before the appointed time. From what Jax could see everyone on his team was already seated and there were another ten guards he didn't know standing around the perimeter of the room with side-arms at their waist. Extra armed guards for his guards? Interesting.

He and Andie found seats that had been saved for them by Isabell Rho and Kirk Chan in front of a small platform. The initiative of the two made him feel better about the leadership team he was going to assemble. Nkosi, also with a sidearm, walked into the room and headed for the platform followed by his aide Walters and two more guards all with arms at their sides. Jax had warned Andie not to be too militaristic but Nkosi seemed to be empowering the idea with armed guards and a show of weapons. It all brought to mind what he had seen with the guards that had taken Larry King from the diner in Luna City.

"I am Musawenkosi Nkosi and Commander in Chief of security for the LMC here on the moon. Your orders have been changed. You are now here to take up the duties of security at the new Aitken Basin mine on the opposite side of this satellite and will depart for that facility at 08:00 tomorrow morning. Before you retire this evening each of you will be issued a small sidearm similar to those you see around the room. You will not load the arms until after the training you will receive at your new station. As a security force you are also here to protect the assets of the mines from attack by alien forces, miners, or civilians; in short, anyone who would destroy the quiet order of our work here. The mine itself will not open for more than 18 months but the infrastructure is in place and over 4,000 people are working to get the facilities operational as soon as they can. Your new commander, Jason Escobar, has been fully briefed on what will be necessary to protect the mines and the facilities from any incursion. Refer all questions you may have to Escobar. Goodnight and welcome to the moon."

He and all his guards departed as quickly as they could and Jax was left to wonder at this new turn. He had not been warned by Tebaldi they would become an armed force. He was trained in small-arms use from other jobs he had along the way but he knew some of his team would have to learn from the beginning how pistols worked. More and more this wasn't what he had signed up for but he needed more time to figure out what would be best for the mines and the citizens of the moon. He was brought out of his reverie by the noise of thirty voices speaking all at once and he stepped onto the small platform and raised his hands for attention. As the uproar settled down, he had a chance to consider what he was about to say.

"For those of you who don't know me, I'm Jason Escobar and the Commander of Security for the new Aitken Basin mine. Amanda Flannigan is my second in command and most of you had a chance to meet her this afternoon. Once we get to Aitken, I'll be making additional assignments of positions to keep us at the best possible operating level. You will all learn the proper use of the firearms to be issued and make sure they are not loaded until training begins."

"We're here to ensure the safety of the mines as well as the safety of the citizens who work in the facilities and colonies supporting the workers in the mine. We are not the enemy of Lunar Freedom or the citizens and I want this team to be a part of the community. The LMC is our employer and we'll protect its assets while protecting the humans who mine the resources that keep the Earth and the system alive. Remember, we are professionals and, as such, will act in the best interest of the people of the solar system. For now, get a good night's sleep and be ready and alert tomorrow morning. It's going to be a long day and I'll have a chance to answer all your questions on the magtube as we head over to Aitken. Dismissed."

The team dispersed and headed for the armory while Jax stood on the platform and thought about his orders. Reginald Tebaldi had been specific that his orders were the only ones that mattered to him. Would he hear from him before they headed out tomorrow and would his orders be different or was Nkosi just a mouthpiece for Joseph Warren, as well? What of Larry King and the man he had spoken to outside the diner? Was the moon on the verge of some sort of revolt? Was Martin Kauri supplying arms to the resistance as well as Lunar Mines personnel? Another long night lay ahead.

Jax was awake early enough to be able to get something to eat before reporting to the magtube at 07:45. As he walked into the mess, he found his team loudly talking over their breakfast about the upcoming assignment and the side arms each had been issued. All of them were smart enough to know the terrible damage a gun fired within the shelter could do if the projectile pierced the outer skin. Each also understood the larger implication of what would happen to a person hit by that projectile. Even among the rookies, there was a feeling their professionalism was in question and they had suddenly ceased being management personnel to somehow become a police force. When they saw Jax the talking eased to a small burble of whispers and slowly died out completely.

"Good morning, team. Welcome to your first day of active duty on the moon. We have about twenty minutes before moving over to the magtube so eat up and start over to the platform."

Jax helped himself to a cup of jolt and a small slice of Luna bread before heading over to the table where Andie was seated with both Rho and Chan. All three started to stand up as he approached but he quickly put a stop to that.

"Sit down, sit down. This isn't the army and you aren't raw recruits. Let's all get one thing straight right now. I'm not a general and this isn't nor will it ever be a military organization. We're a civilian security force and I don't want the miners or the support personnel thinking of us as the enemy. Is that understood?"

"Yes, sir," the three said in unison.

"Good. Enjoy your breakfast. We'll be heading over to the magtube soon. We've got a lot of work to do before we get to Aitken."

Twenty minutes later Jax and his team were assembled waiting for the magtube to arrive. He was pleased to see how professional each member looked as they waited for the transfer. There was very little chatter now and most had retreated into themselves to consider their place in the new organization. Jax hoped they would relax once they were aboard the tube and underway. At that moment the magtube pulled up next to the platform and the umbilicus was extended to connect the platform to the train. The team moved quickly to enter their assigned car and each took a seat awaiting departure. Jax motioned Andie to sit with him a couple of rows ahead of the team. He and Andie were just getting seated when the magtube left the platform and accelerated to full speed quickly enough to push everyone deep into their seats. Jax looked out the window at the magnificent splendor of the lunar landscape of deep grey. It was composed of mixed regolith and boulders from the size of small towns down to pebbles and dust. He knew it could be a cruel and unforgiving environment and he would make surface training one of the team's many priorities.

As he had expected, once they were on their way, the chatter picked up and he could tell the team was more comfortable and looking forward to the new assignment.

"Okay, Andie, I had a chance last night to look over the records of Rho and Chan and I think they will make good junior commanders. You'll be in charge of getting them organized and splitting up the team into two equally experienced groups. Let them know before we get to Aitken so they can begin to take control and start to separate the team."

"I think you're making a good choice Jax, and I know they won't disappoint you. I'll go back and start the ball rolling."

She left Jax to himself and he once again looked out over the unforgiving moonscape before turning to his comm and reviewing the personnel files of each of his team members. He was so engrossed and the magtube was so comfortable it was a surprise when the squawk box announced they would be arriving at Aitken within five minutes. He looked up from his comm just as they crested the high hills that ringed this, the largest impact crater in the solar system.

Jax stood and faced his team.

"This is it. South Pole-Aitken basin. It's was more than 2,500 kilometers in circumference and more than 13 kilometers deep in most spots. From his viewpoint, we couldn't see the other rim because of the short horizon on the moon but he could see the magtube track crossing toward the far horizon and the new base and mine."

"LMC spent a lot of money to open this mine. The ejecta from the impact in this crater carved out such a large amount that it brought the underlying minerals much closer to the surface. We're here to protect the ongoing mining for the various minerals beneath. The mine is designed to support more than fifty thousand people when fully operations. Our job is facilitate that transition smoothly and without any trouble." Suddenly a small group of outbuildings appeared on the horizon and quickly filled the windows as the magtube began to slow for arrival. Three minutes later they pulled next to the South Pole-Aitken Basin platform and came to a stop. The umbilicus attached to the train and people poured out of the other cars and quickly filled the space. Jax's team seemed to be waiting for some sort of acknowledgment from Jax before they departed.

"Okay, here we are. Let's get out on the platform and find our way to the barracks."

The team made an orderly exit and was met by a man holding a sign with Jax's name on it. He made his way over to the man along with his team and said,

"Jason Escobar and the new security team reporting."

"I'm Tanjit Screed, your team secretary and office clerk. I'll take you over to headquarters and let you get your team settled in. Is there anything you need before we start?"

"Thanks, Screed, no. Let's get going."

"Right this way. Welcome to Aitken Basin." Screed said as they proceeded off the platform and into the confines of the lower levels of the support community Jax soon learned was called Coober Luna.

CHAPTER TEN

Screed hurried the team along and out of the platform area which was on the first level below the crust of the moon.

"When you step in say Level 5 and the gravlift will take you to level 5 down."

It only took moments for the team to reassemble on the lower level.

"Just follow me to your new quarters. You'll have a large mess and recreation area and shared accommodation for the team. Mr. Escobar's quarters will be in the small office complex down that hall. His private quarters will be off the conference room."

There were storage facilities, an armory, and two large warehouse areas which also had large freight gravlifts with direct access to the surface. This was the lowest level in this part of the facility and the team could secure the area by closing the gravlift to any unauthorized personnel. Screed took the team to the conference room and stood to one side as everyone assembled. Jax stood and addressed the team,

"Okay, settle down, settle down. Store your gear and report back here in twenty minutes prepared to go topside. I want Flannigan, Rho, and Chan to report back here in ten minutes. Screed, I want a word with you. Dismissed."

Screed walked over to Jax as the team dispersed to find their quarters and get settled in.

"Okay, Screed, I'm going to get the team topside to make sure they can handle the new gee force and function as a team. While we're on the surface I want you to look over the team's files. They've already been uploaded to your comm so you should be able to get us organized by this afternoon. Any questions?"

"No, sir. I'll get to work right away."

Jax went to his quarters and threw his bag on the bed. There would be plenty of time to unpack once he saw how the team could function on the surface.

Ten minutes later, Flannigan, Rho, and Chan appeared at his door.

"Is everyone finding a bunk and getting their gear stowed?"

"Yes, sir. I've also explained to Rho and Chan their responsibilities as squad leaders." Flannigan said as she took a seat along with the other two.

"Why don't we call the two teams Red team and White team? I want to get away, as much as possible, from the military nomenclature. We're a civilian security team working for the LMC on Earth. Our goal is to keep the miners safe and help get the mine up and working. Rho, you'll be in charge of the red team and I want you to watch the group today and select thirteen members by this afternoon. Chan, you'll be in charge of the white team and you'll do the same. That'll leave us with one person over. Take a good look at them today and let me know if we have any goofballs that Flannigan and I will have to work with personally. Okay?"

"Understood, sir. I have a question, however."

"What is it, Rho?"

"Once we've divided the teams out will we be able to break them apart in the barracks? What I mean by that is will I be able to move my team to one part of the area?"

"Of, course. I don't want the two teams to become too competitive,

58

however. Let's keep it nice and friendly so that when needed we can work together. Understood?"

"Yes, sir." both said at once.

"Good, now let's get suited up for the surface. When we get back this afternoon, we'll start the sidearm training."

They rose as one and headed for the storage area where the rest of the team was gathering. Some had already started suiting up and were helping one another to safety check the suits as they were donned. Jax had decided to use the large freight gravlift so the team could get to the surface as one. When everyone was suited and checked he led them to the warehouse area and the lifts.

"Once we get to the surface. we'll start by taking a walk toward the rim hills. I want everyone to stay together as much as possible and help each other when needed. Understood?"

"Yes, sir." The team replied almost in unison. Their voices blended and echoed a little inside Jax's helmet. There was no way to tell one member from another using the radio but Jax hoped they would start to understand how the system worked and keep the chatter down to a minimum.

"Ready. Get on the lift and try not to use the radios too much until we all get used to how they operate. Try not to cut off someone until they've finished talking. I know you've all had training for this but the first time on the surface for some of you will be exciting and I want to keep the team together while we learn about the gee forces and the lunar surface."

The team assembled on the gravlift and Jax pushed the up button. The lift was also an airlock and once they arrived at the surface level the bottom would create a seal similar to that used for personal airlocks.

"Listen up," Jax said. "Once the lift is locked into place, we'll be able to simply walk off the lift and onto the tarmac. From there we'll start their hike and education about the surface of the moon. I plan on us exercising for about four hours."

Jax knew any longer and the team might be too fatigued to be of much use later in the day. Welcome to Coober Luna, he thought.

The brutally incandescent desolation of the moon's surface immediately drew Jax to its unconventional beauty. While his team was getting settled after the ride up to the surface on the freight gravlift, Jax took his time to survey the surroundings. He relished the reality of actually standing on the surface of the satellite that had been circling the Earth for more than 4.5 billion years. The unfiltered sunlight created harsh deep shadows between the low ridges and boulders that littered the ground within the South Pole-Aitken Basin. Everyone on the team was spellbound by the site of the surface. There was no talking and Jax wanted to help them relax.

"Listen up. You are standing in the vacuum that surrounds the moon. At the moment the exterior temperature is 121 degrees Celsius, or 250 degrees Farenheit. Take some time to look around and get a sense of where you are."

Jax could see the team members start looking around, touching helmets to talk, and getting a feel for just where they were.

As inhospitable as it appeared, Jax found the moon's surface beautiful in a rugged and interestingly inviting way. Surprisingly, the close horizon of the moon also gave it a less expansive feeling than many places on Earth. Jax took one last sweeping 360-degree view of the surface and turned to his team.

"Okay, heads up. We're going to walk sixteen kilometers out and back to get used to working on the surface. Stay with the group and don't try to do more than you're comfortable with. Rho and Chan get your squads together and let's get going."

They very quickly formed a group, and Jax started walking south from the base. It was slow going with team members falling behind almost immediately because there had been very little low gravity training before they left the Earth.

"All of you are lucky, you know. These lightweight sheaths are a far cry from the old suits with bulky hinged joints at elbows and knees. The new faceplates are superior to those that didn't allow for any peripheral vision." The new suits were lightweight close-fitting carbon-fiber sheaths with supple joints and a helmet that provided a full wrap-around faceplate. Even the gloves had been slimmed down to allow easy access to tools and accessories which made working on the surface easier. Still, as the team moved out there were occasional stumbles and more than a few falls. Every once in a while, a team member or two would hop off the surface to see how high he or she could jump in the 1/6 gravity.

They moved like that for more than an hour when Jax decided to call a halt and let everyone rest for ten minutes.

"We'll stop here for a rest. Rho and Flannigan meet me here. The rest of you settle down. Use the nipple in your suit for a sip of water. I don't want any of you dehydrating on me."

Rho and Flannigan arrived and Jax touched their helmet with his.

"Switch to channel six," he said. "We'll head for the far horizon for about another hour, then head back. Flannigan, use your GPS to locate us and head us in the right direction when we turn back."

He turned to look at the tracks his team had left on the surface and marveled at the precise indentations each of their boots had made as they dwindled back in the direction from which they had come. He couldn't see the base but knew the GPS would help take them back to their starting point even though it had fallen below the short horizon on the moon. He turned his head, found the nipple, and took a sip of water. He found it hard not to enjoy the view and once again turned a complete 360 degrees to take in the vista.

"Sir, anything else?" Rho said. Jax realized he had been lost in his own thoughts and quickly came back to the here and now.

"I'm amazed at the complexity of the surface's granular regolith and the sparkling bits of mica and other reflective minerals embedded with the flat dust that mixes with everything we see."

Slowly he turned back to his team and selected the announce button on his interior face panel which would allow him to talk to everyone at once. The chatter from the team had increased after stopping and had now reached a point that had everyone stepping on each other's transmissions to create a loud and unintelligible babble.

"Heh, heh, settle down," Jax said loudly. It still took a while for everyone to stop talking.

"Okay, keep the chatter down to a minimum. If you want to speak to a single person just touch your helmets together and mute the radio. If you need to speak to Rho, Chan, or me, use the assigned frequency; channel six. Now, let's keep moving. Most of you seem to have gotten the rhythm needed to move along the surface so I'm going to increase our speed over the next hour. Let's move out."

He had them moving at a faster pace and there was less horse-play among the team than there had been the first hour. They were able to reach the waypoint Jax had set into his positioner in less than forty minutes.

"We've all done a great job of learning how to work on the surface. Now, let's head back to base." Jax turned them around and started the journey back to base. They had passed a low mound of rubble coming out and Jax decided to let them try hiking up one side and down the other.

"Team, we're going to head up that small hill. Remember your training and what you've learned since we've been on the surface."

He led them up the incline and when they reached the top he stopped to let them enjoy the higher point of view. In fact, from this height, it was possible to see the low-rise domes of the Aitken base.

He had just started the team down when a body, with arms and legs flailing, flew past him in a long arc from behind. Everyone came to a stop and Jax knew at once the team member was going to hit the ground with much more force than expected. Although the gravity was light, everyone still maintained the same mass as when on Earth. By throwing himself off the top the team member had initiated a trajectory that would take him to the base of the rise but at a speed far higher than was safe. It only took moments for the man to hit the surface and try to absorb the hard hit he was taking. He collapsed face-first with out-stretched arms onto the unforgiving regolith and his helmet exploded in a burst of plasteel and debris. The arms and legs kicked violently once then a moment later with far less force. It was all over in less than twenty seconds. He lay there not moving and Rho was the first to start down the rise with Chan, Jax, and Andie right behind. For several seconds there wasn't a sound over the comms then the team irrupted into a cacophony of shouts, explicative grunts, and demands to save him.

"It's Jackson, sir, he's been testing his limits since we came out. He's the one that was doing all the jumping and hopping around as he got more comfortable with the suit and the gravity." Rho said as she reached the sprawled-out man. The team's shouts stopped as she bent over the immobile form and slowly rolled him toward her. His faceplate was shattered and the vacuum that surrounded the moon had sucked the air out of his suit and his body. He was a frozen lifeless form. Rho stood up, pushed the surrounding team back from the corpse, and faced Jax.

"He's dead, sir. The helmet shattered on impact and he must have died within moments."

A rumble started to form from the team's headsets and Jax put his hand in the air and shouted to overcome the chatter.

"Hold it, hold it. Settle down, now. Rho, select a small team and take the body back to Coober Luna. We'll push on and you follow up as soon as you can."

"Aye, sir." Rho pointed to two other team members and the three moved down to Jackson's inert form.

As the impact of the sudden tragedy settled over the team the chatter stayed subdued as Jax led them back to Aitken base. He decided not to say anything until they had a chance to get out of their surface suits and had assembled in the rec area. The trip back went quickly without further incident and the team was shortly gathered to hear what Jax would say.

"We've been on the surface for more than four hours and most of you are dehydrated. Get something to drink and we'll wait for Rho and her group to get back before we review what just happened."

Thirty minutes later the team, less Jackson, was fully assembled and Jax stood up to address them all.

"I'm sure Jackson was a good man but he became too confident in his ability to handle the gravity. He forgot about his mass and how once accelerated, it might be more difficult to stop. It's a tragedy he had to pay for with his life. For the most part, each of you handled yourself on the surface and will, I believe, have no trouble if we need to operate there. Get some rest this afternoon and evening. We're going to full scheduling tomorrow and I want this team to get to know the mine and the support areas like the back of your hand. Dismissed."

Most of the team left the rec area and Jax motioned to Andie to stay behind.

"That was a nasty piece of business out there and a very hard lesson for the team to learn so early. I want to make sure it doesn't happen again so set up additional training sessions with smaller groups over the next few weeks."

"Yes, sir. I would also like to suggest we train the team inside to ensure they can work at peak performance whatever might happen."

"What are you worried about, Andie?"

"Since we've arrived, I've heard from friends of mine who've been living here for many years. They say the miners are on edge and don't believe the LMC is abiding by the safety rules set up before this mine was opened. Lunar Freedom is calling a meeting in three days to talk about possible work actions starting as soon as next week. If they decided to strike, LMC is going to go ballistic and there'll be demands for us to make them go back to work. It could get really ugly very quickly. Even though this is a new team, we can get them up to speed soon enough if we train a little more now."

"Okay, set up the scheduling, and let's take a small group to the Lunar Freedom meeting. I met a member on Earth just before I left and he seemed genuinely interested in the welfare of the miners and the safety of the mine. We'll see what he and the miners have to say."

"Thanks, Jax, I'll get started this afternoon and I'll select the team we'll want at the meeting."

Andie left Jax alone in the rec area and he looked around the space. There were a couple of small groups of men and women having hushed conversations and Jax was sure they were talking about the frightening accident on the surface.

CHAPTER ELEVEN

The following nine months were a whirlwind of activity for Jax and his new team. They worked to become a cohesive and effective security team while learning how to be a part of the community of Coober Luna and Aitken Base. Jax also made a point of going out alone to meet the men and women working on the base. He started at one of the favorite hangouts of the miners. The Rusty Pick was just the type of bar one would expect. Cheap beer and shots. The crowd was noisy and the music loud. People didn't dance so much as move around and yell at each other. Every once in a while, Jax would overhear part of a conversation that included words like, rebellion, freedom, money, LMC, and a mix of patois all spoken with the same feeling. He would often sit at the bar and eventually he would strike up a conversation.

"I'm Jax, how's it goin'?"

The man turned to him, stared, then smiled.

"Okay for an old miner. You new to the moon?"

"I've been here almost a year. You say you're a miner, tell me about that, please."

"Have been all my life. I've been in this particular hole eighteen months."

"Why do you call it a hole. It's a state-of-the-art mine."

"Bullshit. LMC cuts every corner they can. It's all smoke and mirrors. They don't care about safety and one day soon hundreds will die."

"That's hard. Where are they failing to protect the mine and the miners?"

"Seals fail, walls collapse, oxygen levels drop without warning. Oh, hell, I could go on but I'm here to get drunk and forget I might die at any moment." He stood up, turned and walked away.

Jax watched him leave and wondered what else he might hear in other bars and clubs.

Other times he would meet up with Andie in a more salubrious venue. Here, too, he heard about the inequities on the moon. The wealth that was being stripped away and how little return the Lunatics received.

They were sitting at a small table when a woman approached, and stood before them.

"I hear you're asking all sorts of questions about the mines. You want to start a rebellion or something. Exactly what do ya' want?"

"Information more than anything else. Would you have a seat and tell us about your job here in Aitken?"

"I work clerical."

"What does that job entail?"

"I balance the amount of ore mined to that which is shipped to Earth or one of the orbiting smelters. My office resolves any discrepancies that might occur."

"What do you and your colleagues think about all the talk of rebellion or mine shutdown?"

"It ain't part of my job to think. I do my job, get paid and that's about it."

"Do you plan to return to Earth any time soon?"

"Who can afford to go back to Earth? I'm lucky to have food on the table for my three kids, water for them to drink and oxygen to breathe."

"Do you think you might join a group hoping to take the moon away from LMC?"

She looked at the two of them and abruptly stood.

"You two work for LMC, don't ya? Ya' ain't gettin' nothing else out of me."

She left them and Andie looked at Jax.

"Not everything on the moon is paradise, is it?"

After months of this, Jax was far more informed about the moon, LMC, the Lunatics and the work he now knew he would be expected to do. On a recent outing, he and Isabell Rho talked about what he had seen and heard.

"Hanging around you has certainly expanded my ideas of what the moon is and what it can be. The Lunatics seem to have valid reasons to be fearful for their life. They also don't like the iniquities between those who work and LMC that only takes."

"Be careful, you'll begin to sound like a rebellious Lunatic."

"Well, I've learned enough that I just might be."

"Have you been attending Freedom meetings?"

"Yea, and I'll continue. It's one of the best ways to know what the Lunatics might do next. I guess we can't join them, but I'm tempted. I guess I need to think about that some more. Still, my mind is open to what they have to say."

"You look worried, Jax. What's going on?"

"Like you, I've heard so much in the past months. I've spoken to waitresses, bar tenders, women with children, men in the mines, and hundreds of others who wanted their say. The moon isn't what I thought it was going to be. The unrest is almost palpable and I am convinced trouble is coming. How do we protect the citizens, the mines and our team?"

Neither said a word as they reached for the Jovian beer.

CHAPTER TWELVE

At Aitken they worked to become a cohesive and effective security team while learning how to be a part of the community of Coober Luna and Aitken Base. Jax was able to meet with Martin often during the period and he enjoyed being at Luna City and its many diversions. He particularly enjoyed the Solar Club which utilized the same inertial suppression technology as transport ships throughout the system. Upon entering the club, one was subjected to full one gee gravity just like Earth, which allowed for unfettered physical activity without the need to be constantly aware of one's weight or mass. The club's amenities included a large and welcoming reception area as well as game rooms and a restaurant that overlooked the swimming pool. There was also a group of tennis courts that helped keep Jax fit for the possible return to Earth for meetings at the LMC headquarters. The whole club was covered by a reinforced plasteel dome tinted to filter out the harmful radiation from the sun.

It was during a visit to the club to celebrate the anniversary of Jax's first year on the moon that he and Martin had their first conversation about the infrastructure of the Aitken mine as well as the overall safety of all the inhabitants of the moon. They were sitting by the pool enjoying a light lunch when Martin's association with Lunar Freedom and Chuck Breckman became the subject.

"When I met Chuck Breckman on Earth," Jax said, "he was working with the LMC to upgrade the security and safety measures for Aitken mine and the other mines around the system. I've met with him at Aitken a few times over the past months and he's still concerned. Lunar Freedom continues to threaten a strike but nothing has come of it so far. To be honest, I'm concerned, as well. It's not just the miners who are in jeopardy, it's my team and the civilian population who'll be in harm's way should anything fail. We've all seen structural inconsistencies within the mine as well as the support facility. There are over 4,000 men and women at Coober Luna and a sudden decompression could kill hundreds, if not thousands."

"Chuck and I meet every time I come to the moon," Martin said.

"I know you are aware of the unrest among the residents and the meetings that have been going on both here in Luna City as well as Aitken Mine. Jax, there is going to be a time when Lunar Mines and the Lunatics will clash. It will probably start with a strike but if LMC doesn't meet Lunar Freedom's demands there's bound to be trouble. Chuck and his group are fully prepared to shut down all mining activity until LMC upgrades the safety issues throughout the system."

"That's going to put me smack in the middle of any trouble that happens. I've been keeping track of the groups that are meeting both here and at Aitken and I know how close we are to a total shutdown. What have you been supplying to Lunar Freedom?"

"That which is needed to ensure they are successful with their fight. I don't want you to get hurt, but I can't stop now. There are enough arms to keep any force now on the moon at bay. I tell you this only because the strike is going to happen soon. If you want to keep your team safe, keep them out of Lunar Freedom's way."

"You know I'm going to have to report this to my superiors, don't you? It's my job to protect the assets of the mines."

71

"Jax, don't you see Lunar Mines is the bad guy here? We, on the moon, need to be able to live our lives without the danger of being killed at any moment. Now is the time for us to throw off the shackles of the corporation and make our own rules. The moon is one of the largest untapped natural resources in the solar system. We are the ones who should be reaping its wealth, not Lunar Mines. The inhabitants are the ones living here and most will never go back to the Earth because they've lived here too long without maintaining the strength needed to return to full gravity. We're lucky; we work for LMC and enjoy benefits most can only dream of. Now is the time for Lunatics to unite and overthrow Lunar Mines' control of our destiny."

Jax was thunderstruck by his words. They had never spoken so candidly to one another and for a moment he was too angry and confused to reply. Finally, he turned to him and said,

"Martin, you know I love you, but I can't stand by and watch while the job I was sent to do is swept away. If this strike occurs, I know I'll be instructed to break it. LMC will send a much larger security force to keep control and that will mean many more people will be in danger."

"Jax, my darling, we have the whole population behind us. The mines and bases all over the moon will stand against Lunar Mines. I know there will be bloodshed but it's the price we are all willing to pay."

"But you live on the Earth, Martin. Why have you gotten involved with this rebellion?"

"The moon is only the tip of the iceberg of the control Lunar Mines exerts throughout the solar system. It's not right to subjugate workers to a life without hope of reaping even a small part of the wealth taken every moment from the mines all over the system. The miners are entitled to more and they intend to take what is rightfully theirs. If Lunar Mines had made the mineworkers partners long ago this wouldn't be happening. They didn't, and now the only way to regain a portion of the wealth earned is to fight the hand that once fed them. Now, however, Lunar Mines charges for water, air, housing, and food while not paying enough for the men and women who work here a chance to leave or even stop working. It's not right and we're going to stop it. I wish I could make you understand. I want you to come with me to the meeting tonight of Lunar Freedom and the citizens of Lunar City. Will you do that for me?"

"That would put my job in jeopardy. Besides, I'm part of the security force and I might not be welcome. And I still don't know if rebellion is the right thing for the Lunatics to consider."

"I've already told Chuck I was going to bring you tonight. He'll make sure you're able to listen to what is going to be said without them trying to tear you apart," he said smiling.

Jax knew he was taking a step that might change the way he thought about the moon and its citizens but he needed to know what was going on and how he and his team would fit into whatever happened.

"Let's go back to the hotel. I'll change into something nondescript and hopefully I won't be recognized."

"That, my dear, is impossible. Almost everyone on the moon knows who you are. They're waiting to be able to share with you their very real concerns and hope you will join them."

That evening he and Martin went into Luna City and the meeting that might change everything for Jax.

"Settle down, settle down!" Charlemagne "Chuck" Breckman shouted as he pounded a small wooden gavel on the table set on a stage raised about 24 inches above the floor of the rec center. It had been turned into a meeting room for the Lunar Freedom event. He continued to use the gavel and slowly the people in the room turned their attention to Chuck and the small group seated with him on the dais. They were meeting in the Luna City headquarters of Lunar Mines and more than three thousand people had arrived to air their grievances and hear what their neighbors and co-workers had to say about the current conditions for workers and residents of the moon. Jax, Andie, and Martin had arrived about three minutes before Chuck started calling for order and hadn't had a chance to speak to any of the attendees. Jax decided to wait until after the meeting to linger with the crowd and listen to the conversations that were bound to follow.

"Okay, okay, please sit down so we can get started. I'm Charlemagne Breckman but most of you know me as Chuck and I'm the chairman of Lunar Freedom which is working to ensure safety in the mines and within the support facilities. My latest experience is not encouraging. The CEO of Lunar Mines, Joseph Warren, is not inclined to change any of the standards that are now in place. Because of that, we have lost more than three hundred of our brothers and sisters in accidents in the past eight months.

"I see Jason Escobar, head of security at Aitken base for LMC, at the back of the room. Jax, come up here and tell us what you can about the current situation?Jason was caught by surprise at his request and slowly moved to the front of the room and the small platform that had been raised. He mounted the steps and faced the crowd.

"I can't speak for Musawenkosi Nkosi, overall chief of security on the moon, but I can tell you Aitken base security has investigated the accidents that occurred at Coober Luna, and at no time were corporate guidelines ignored or changed. The accidents have all been proven to be just that, accidents, and no one person is responsible. All were a domino effect of single small incidents that ultimately turned into a larger situation. My team at Aitken base continually monitors our situation and we will continue to help ensure the safety of all the residents of that facility."

He left the platform and joined Andie at the back of the room. As he was walking away Chuck took the microphone and started listing the accidents that had occurred at the Tycho base mine that continued to kill a few people at a time and were somehow considered employee fault.

"These are just a few examples of what has happened all over the moon. An auxiliary airlock failed when four men were preparing to leave the mine and exit to the surface during the performance of their duties. The pod door on a rover unexpectedly broke from its hinges while a team of seven was on the surface moving excess equipment into the storage bay. That incident killed three when the door hit them and the other four who had been in the pod without helmets on. An unattended rover inexplicably started moving across the surface and crushed three miners relocating a sensitive pathway marker while more than four kilometers away from Luna City. In each instance, LMC declared the accidents unavoidable but each was later found to have been caused by man-made faults. Two investigators are calling it sabotage or worse, murder."

"Escobar knows about the accidents here in Luna City and he's been lucky enough not to have had the same types of deaths at Coober Luna. It's also important to understand we are at their mercy. If they don't find out the answers, we are going to have to do it ourselves."

The room erupted in yells of "yes!", "let's get them!", "down with Lunar Mines!", "down with Warren!", and many, many more. Finally, Chuck raised his hands in an attempt to quiet the room. Once again, the space slowly resumed some order and he continued.

"We have finally reached a point where we are unable to live as we might please. Air, water, accommodation, and food all cost more than any of us make from the mines. When we try to leave, we are told we don't have the funds to return to Earth and will have to continue to work until we save enough. LMC knows we can't save enough with what we are paid and are now simply slaves to the corporation. It's time we made some changes. The population of the moon is over 750,000 men, women, and children. Of that number more than 400,000 are employed by Lunar Mines and are living from hand to mouth. The gross lunar product is more than 957 billion credits a year and more than 85 percent of that money goes into the pockets of Lunar Mines. They are raping the moon, and us, in their unfettered greed. It's time we stood up to them and asked for only what is due us. Better working conditions with better wages and guaranteed return passage to Earth any time we want."

The room erupted again and Chuck just let them yell. He knew they would eventually vote to strike against LMC and it was only a matter of time. With his speech Chuck set the ball rolling and he knew it wouldn't be long until a full rebellion would occur. His dream was for a free and independent moon trading with partners all around the solar system and hopefully one day to the stars. Redirecting the wealth of the moon to the citizens would help make that dream a reality. He also knew it was a dangerous idea and that many Lunatics might die. He had to figure out a way to force Lunar Mines' hand into turning over the moon to the Lunatics. For Chuck, nothing less would do.

Chuck stepped from the platform and was immediately surrounded by a small group of people all wanting to say something to him. The majority of others started drifting away in a cloud of loud talk and gestures and suggestions they take this conversation to the nearest bar. Slowly the room became very quiet and finally, Chuck was alone except for Jax, Andie, and Martin.

"What are you doing, Chuck? You almost started a riot. If you continue to call for rebellion there's going to be trouble. You know that, don't you?" said Andie.

"I know, but trouble is what we need on this rock. We have no say over our lives and LMC continues to ignore our requests for meetings. The only way to get their attention is to go on strike. I promise it will be non-violent unless LMC decides to take it further. If they do, we may force their hand and ban them from the moon. We'll take control of the mines and we'll create a manufacturing industry on the moon that will not need the help of the Earth to survive."

"So, you would like to see an independent moon. Will you then take your revolution to the planets?" Jax said with what he hoped was a joke.

"Of course, it's the only step we can take. No one should be forced to be a slave for a corporation that doesn't care about a person's life or security. It's what I've hoped for since I first came to Luna."

"I can't say I didn't see this coming, Martin. "We've talked enough for me to understand your feelings. So you and the Breckman brothers expect to form a militia and overthrow LMC."

"Of course, Jax. Don't you see we're ready to stand on our own? Dr. Paul Darwin has created a new chip that is superior to anything now in use and will transform information and even warfare. Dr. Darwin's is isskes We've been using them secretly for more than three years. It will create a manufacturing base for us and, at the same time, free us from our ties to the Earth. Water and air are already made here and we grow all of our food. We don't need the Earth and now's the time to show them so."

"The moon itself will became the vehicle through which information was passed. It's also undetectable to any other type of communications assembly. Dr. Darwin has created the ultimate chip and it will work on the Earth, any other planet in the solar system and he believes anywhere in the galaxy. They will be manufactured on the moon more inexpensively than anywhere in the galaxy and will guarantee independence for the satellite one day."

"Okay, Chuck, I'll go along with you as long as there is no violence. I'll keep my team at Aitken unless ordered otherwise."

"Thanks. Now, if you'll excuse me, I want to join my team at the *Rusty Flange* for a drink and more conversation about tonight's meeting."

He walked away and Jax, Andie, and Martin were standing alone in the now empty rec room.

"Jax, I told you there was going to be trouble. We're not military; we're a civilian security force and we shouldn't be getting involved in this mess." Andie said.

"Sorry, Andie, we're in it up to our necks. I don't want to do anything to upset Lunar Freedom and we won't confront them unless specifically ordered to interfere. Even then, I want to keep injuries to a minimum. So, have the team unload their sidearms and keep the ammo separate but handy. Anything else?"

"Nothing else, boss, but try to keep us out of the action, if you can."

"See you back at base."

After Andie left, Jax turned to Martin.

"I should have known you would get me into trouble. I need to tell you something, as well. From the moment I took this job, I have been getting orders from Reginald Tebaldi which contradicted the orders I get from Moose Nkosi. So far, I've been able to work without either one knowing what I'm doing. The strike will make my job much more difficult. At some point, I'll have to take sides and that's unsettling for me and my team. I don't know what they think of all this and I need to find out. Things are sure going to get messy."

"Jax, my love, you'll have to break away at some point. The future is here and now; not back on Earth. Nkosi will side with LMC because he's under their control. So far, you've been able to escape their scrutiny but once this news gets out, they will come for you and expect you to obey them. That's when the break will occur. You'll need to be strong, my dear, and I know you will be."

Jax looked at Martin for a moment then grabbed him by the shoulders, pulled him closer, and began to kiss him. He fell into his embrace and together they stood like that for a long time. They finally separated and walked out of the rec room and toward the Luna Metropole where they were staying.

CHAPTER THIRTEEN

"Chuck, what the hell do you think you're doing?" Jax asked. "Lunar Mines won't meet your demands and will probably fire all of you. When do you plan to notify the LMC of the strike?" He and Chuck were communicating via face comm and Jax was hoping he couldn't see how upset he was.

"The strike is called for next Wednesday at 07:00. It gives us just five days to finish the preparations."

"What are you going to be asking the residents to do?"

"Lunar Freedom is calling for every miner and mine employee to stay off work beginning that day until Lunar Mines meet our demands for higher wages, lower rent, air, and water costs, and guaranteed passage back to Earth once contractual agreements were met."

"Everyone working for LMC signs a 24-month contract which is renewed from year to year. We propose that the agreement be amended to include a six-month clause that allows the worker to leave after that time with no loss of benefits should he or she desire. We also want each miner to be allowed to share 5 percent of the profits from all the production of the moon for the previous year. The profits would be allocated to Lunar Freedom and the citizens of the moon."

"You know Lunar Mines won't like the ultimatum when they received notice of the strike and you'll have to wait for a reaction."

"They already know. We sent the ultimatum at midnight last night.

We had already formulated our demands and it was just a matter of timing. Now, we wait and see. For the moment LMC has not replied. Also, they can't fire us, Jax. If they fire us, who will they get to work the mines? Every miner and citizen voted for this strike and no one will break it. Next Wednesday the mines will shut down until we reach an understanding."

"What if LMC decides to send a team of security up here to force people back to work? Are you prepared for that kind of confrontation?"

"We are prepared for every contingency they might throw at us. We'll take over the Central Control offices today and allow no one in but members of Lunar Freedom. We're also going to take over the smaller control facilities spread throughout Luna. We plan to keep control so they can't cut off air and water. As an added precaution we stockpiled food and water for more than a week in all the locations. We'll be okay."

"You've really done it, you know. I'm caught in the middle. I've come to love the moon and the outrageous extreme beauty of the surface. I like the people here and I think my team feels the same way. Headquarters is going to have another take on this. They will instruct me and my team to get people back to work. I hope I can do that without violence. By the way, how has Martin outfitted your band of rebels?"

"We're prepared to meet whatever LMC throws at us and we'll do everything we can to protect the assets of the mines. After all, we expect them to be part of our financial future, as well."

"You didn't answer my question. What has Martin given to you to stop any extra security forces?"

"Jax, I'm not going to tell you that until you make up your mind where you stand on this. It might be time for you to think about what is going to happen. I know you've been on the moon less than a year, but you understand how things work around here and you see the injustice.

Think about it and make a choice. Find out what your team thinks of the strike and how it might end for Lunar Mines and themselves." Chuck said as he broke the connection.

Jax looked at the comm and thought about what had been said. Where were his loyalties? He had been drifting more and more toward an understanding of the miners and the Lunatics in general. They had valid points and Lunar Mines refused to negotiate.

Jax still had work to do at Aiken base but he kept thinking about the Lunatics and what might happen when the strike started. He kept busy in an attempt to ease his concerns.

He was working with Andie and six of his team on the surface to survey locations for small arms emplacements should they become necessary. The moon and the Earth had each turned their dark side toward one another and Jax stared in wonder at the bejeweled orb above. The terminator on Earth had just crossed the western coast of North America and the illumination from hundreds of millions of lights dazzled even from almost 400,000 kilometers away. From Earth, the moon was in the phase called new and it was between the sun and the Earth with Tycho Base and Luna City in darkness for about another week. Jax loved this phase almost as much as the full phase and he often thought there was no time he didn't like being on the moon. He realized he had come to love the ever-changing beauty of the landscape and the thrilling sense of adventure it offered. Enough, he thought, time to get to work even though I probably will side with the miners when the time comes.

"Andie, let's go toward the hills in that direction about one hundred meters and place the last of the armaments there."

"Okay, Jax. Williams, Osama, and Choo bring the carryall this way and the rest of you follow me, and let's get the last installation in place."

The team turned toward the hills and had just begun to move when a very large, ovoid-shaped vessel burst over the close horizon quickly followed by three more and finally six vessels to make a small armada of ten ships. Within seconds they were slowing over Tycho base and the surrounding area. The size and proximity of the vessels blotted out Jax's view of the Earth with dark shadows playing all around his team and the base.

"What the heck is that? Flannigan, hold where you are. Team, gather around her position."

This left Jax standing alone about fifty meters from his team and between them and the base. He watched as the vessels slowed to a complete stop and hovered over the area. They were like nothing Jax had ever seen. He realized they were more elliptical than ovoid as he had first thought and were symmetrical from his point of view. Jax switched his comm to central control and was about to speak when his speaker burst out.

"All personnel this is the civilian command. This is not a drill. Emergency teams to stations, all others remain where you are. Every access point will be secured and there will be no access to the surface. All surface teams return to base immediately. This is not a drill."

Jax and his team had not been the only surface workers at the time and he watched as the other teams began to move toward the base and the airlocks.

"Flannigan, move the team back to base. I'll follow with the carryall. Now, move."

His team quickly responded to his orders and Jax was happy to see them start their return to base. He began to move toward the carryall when he was surrounded by a blaze of white light from the ship directly above. He watched as a small ship exited from the larger and dropped to the surface. His team had almost reached the base airlock and he watched to make sure they were in no danger. The small ship descended to within ten meters of his position and touched the regolith with the slightest puff as its pods sought the stability of the surface. Slowly an opening appeared at the side of the vessel which Jax now realized was twenty to twenty-five meters in length. That also made the ship from which it had come much larger than he had thought. A figure in a spacesuit similar to his exited the craft and began to walk toward Jax. It was obvious the figure was used to working in the one-sixth gravity of the moon as its movements were sure and direct. As the figure approached, Jax looked hard at the visor but the sun shield was activated and he couldn't see inside the helmet. He couldn't understand why he hadn't wanted to flee and his only excuse was his extreme interest in the ships, the small shuttle, and the figure that was now directly in front of him. It stopped and stood for a moment seeming to look at Jax and decide what its next move would be.

Slowly the sun shield began to clear and Jax was able to make out the interior and who was within. Astoundingly, it was Martin Kauri.

"Martin! What are you doing here and where did those ships come from?"

Jax could see he didn't hear him so he leaned over to touch his helmet.

"Martin, what are you doing here and where did those ships come from? Why don't you have your comm on?"

"I don't want everyone at Tycho Base or Aitken to know who or what is in those ships. I want you to come aboard with me. We have so much to discuss and there is someone aboard you will want to meet."

Jax started to reply but Martin had already started moving toward the small shuttle and expected Jax to follow him. The portal was still open and he stepped inside with Jax on his heels. The opening closed and he followed Martin to the front of the ship and its helm.

"Strap in, Jax." He said as he touched the flight screen and began the process of lifting them from the surface and returning to the larger ship. Within moments they were off the satellite and headed back to the same opening Jax had seen when the ships first arrived. Quickly they entered the opening and it closed behind them as Martin deftly let the shuttle float above the opening until it closed after which he settled the shuttle to the now solid deck. He made a few touches on the screen and turned to Jax as he took off his helmet.

"You can remove your helmet and suit once you exit the shuttle, the atmosphere is Earth normal."

Martin moved toward the exit portal, stepped down to the deck, and walked away toward what looked like the control module for this area of the larger ship.

Jax followed after removing his helmet and exiting the craft. He realized gravity had returned as the shuttle touched down. His heart was beating as if he had just run the 100-meter dash and he began to take long deep breaths to adjust his breathing and heartbeat to a more normal pace.

After a few moments, he was able to look around and inspect his surroundings. He was standing on a deck which overlooked a large area in which there were numerous smaller ships and other equipment that suggested this was a hanger of some sort. As he surveyed the area, he also became aware of a series of viewports about ten meters above the decking and in which he could see humanoid figures jostling for a closer view of the hanger and him.

Jax caught up with Martin next to the secondary airlock and storage area to find Martin peeling out of his suit and he quickly followed his lead. These modern space suits were far easier to remove and don and they were out of them within minutes.

"Okay, tell me what's going on and where did these ships come from?"

"All in good time. Come with me, now, I have someone I want you to meet."

They went to a gravlift and ascended more than ten decks to the highest level on the ship. There, Martin exited and turned to the left, followed by Jax. He didn't know where they were going but it was obvious to him this was a type of ship never before seen in the solar system. They approached a door that slid open before Martin reached it and waited while Jax followed behind. They were in a conference room which, from the look of it, was just rear of the bridge of the ship.

"Jax, come on in. You know Chuck Breckman and this is Dr. Carson Darwin. Have a seat, we have much to discuss." Martin almost commanded.

"Dr. Darwin is the developer of these ships you are so interested in. I had them produced on a small platform orbiting the Earth with the Delhi Five transfer station. Lunar Mines paid for their construction but Warren knows nothing of their existence. As you guessed, my interest in Lunar Freedom and my desire to see the moon freed from the tyranny of Lunar Mines forced me to take action on my own. Over the past four years, Dr. Darwin has overseen the construction of these ships and I have seen to it they are armed and very dangerous. Warren will stop at nothing to retain his control of the mines throughout the system and I intend to be part of the force that stops him."

"Martin approached me five years ago with his plan to build and use these ships when the time came," Chuck interjected. "Lunar Freedom worked with him and Dr. Darwin to train as many men and women as needed to man the ships and operate the armaments. We are prepared for whatever Warren throws at us once the strike starts."

"Where does that leave me? You know Warren will send more security troops our way as soon as shipments from the moon have stopped. I have orders to stop the strike and make the employees go back to work. Reginald Tebaldi has also instructed me to reorganize the security teams already on the moon in preparation for the arrival of four hundred more team members. When the strike starts, I am to arrest Nkosi and his close advisors and throw them in the brig. He won't like that and there are members of his team that will try to stop me. Things will start to go downhill very fast from there."

"That's where my small armada of ships comes in, Jax. We're prepared to confront Warren's new security forces with a larger and more lethal force than they have ever imagined. Dr. Darwin, with my help, has fitted these ships with the most revolutionary armaments and defenses available. With the use of tachyon waves and a matter/anti-matter pulse bomb, we can stop any ship from crossing our web of defense. Like a large fishing net, the web is dispersed along any plane we select. It can be adjusted to any angle and can protect anything from crossing its boundaries. The web incapacitates any propulsion system and disarms any weapons aboard the ships that try to cross. Warren's men and women will have nothing like it and we will be able to force them to surrender to our demands."

"Warren and Tebaldi must have known something about these ships because my last communication said the new teams would also have armaments not seen on the moon before. He didn't elaborate so I don't know what to expect."

"At this point, it doesn't matter what they throw at us. We're going on strike and ultimately detaching ourselves from the rule of Lunar Mines, the LMC, and Joseph Warren." Chuck declared. "What we need to know, Jax is whether or not you're with us or against us."

"Oh, I'm with you, alright. Let's get a plan in place that uses my small team, as well. They are more than ready to rip this satellite out of the hands of Lunar Mines and the Earth."

Jax was convinced now that Warren had to be stopped and he must somehow help Chuck and the Lunar Freedom membership take over the mines for the good of all. That would also make Chuck, with the help of Jax and Martin, the person to lead the Lunatics into the future.

CHAPTER FOURTEEN

"Comm, connect me to Moose Nkosi." Reginald prepared himself for this encounter and what he would say to Nkosi. The connection was quickly made and within moments Moose was on the screen.

"Mr. Tebaldi, how can I help you today?" he said after a moment's hesitation.

"Hello, Moose, it's what I can do for you I want to talk about. I know the strike is imminent and Warren's office will be sending out instructions today on how to handle the strikers. Ignore his instructions. I have new orders and they will help us all maintain control of the mines and keep the miners working for our good."

"Before you start, there is a development you should be made aware of. Someone, we don't know who yet, has control of a fleet of ten vessels which are very large, very maneuverable and, we believe, armed. They arrived this morning and took Jason Escobar aboard. He was released after about thirty minutes and returned to his unit on the surface. While the vessels were stationed over Tycho base we tried to scan them but everything we used was jammed. We believe they are part of a new force working with Lunar Freedom to overthrow Lunar Mines and take control of the moon."

"My most recent report did not include that information. Where are they now?" Reginald said with a firm voice.

"They pulled back from the moon and at the moment we have not been able to locate them. But I don't believe they went far."

"Lunar Mines is sending a force of twelve ships with more than eighteen hundred mercenary soldiers to bring control to the moon. They will be leaving Blythe Space Port this afternoon and should arrive at the moon thirty-six hours later. I want you and Escobar to meet them when they land. They are instructed to report to you and follow your orders. They have been trained and are prepared to force the workers back into the mines. They are also instructed to shoot to kill, if necessary. Do you understand?"

"Are you sure this is the way you want this to play out?" Moose said.

"Do not try to change my plans. The force is under my command and Warren is unaware I have given the commander's instructions that countermand his. Once the moon is under my control, I'll kick Warren off the board of directors and become the new Chairman of Lunar Mines. Get your men ready for the arrival of the army that will bring the moon into my hands."

Nkosi's face was alive with uncontrolled emotions and when he spoke his voice was deep and very quiet.

"You're sure this is what you want for the moon? A force the size you are sending might not be able to control the miners. There are over 750,000 people on the moon right now and many of them will join the miners in an attempt to take control of their satellite."

"This force is just the beginning. I am sending more than twenty thousand follow-up mercenaries within the next seven days. This is the force that Warren thinks he is controlling. In fact, my team will be in charge of the new troopers when they arrive. Everything is under control. Just follow my orders. Do you understand?"

"You realize this could go terribly wrong, don't you? We know nothing of the ten ships that appeared and are now somewhere in the vicinity. We should be careful about how we proceed."

"Enough! Take control of the new team when it arrives and prepare them for the arrival of the rest of the force." Tebaldi said as he ended the communication.

Reginald Tebaldi leaned back in his chair which was in the break-fast nook of his condominium high above level 21 of New Manhattan. The building was on the east side of the platform and rose high above the Atlantic Ocean. He had an expansive view of what had been Long Island before global warming pushed sea levels more than twenty meters above what had been the high tide mark in the early 2000s. When the ice from both polar caps finished melting seventy percent of old Manhattan was awash and the creation of New Manhattan had begun. Now, three hundred years later, the metropolis was raised above the ocean with twenty lower levels beneath the platform that now supported the new city.

"Comm, connect me to Altair on *Mademoiselle Rouge.*"

Tebaldi knew his moment had come. Within two days Lunar Freedom would call a halt to all activity in the mines and demand a change in the way the miners were paid and how they were treated while in the employ of Lunar Mines. It was the turn of events Reginald had planned for in the five years he had worked for Joseph Warren. He had amassed a fortune in cash, mineral rights, property, and businesses throughout the solar system. With it all, he had assembled a team he believed would see his every desire to rule the moon and the colonies realized. The *Mademoiselle Rouge* was his private space yacht berthed at the Teterboro spaceport just outside New Manhattan. He was convinced Warren knew nothing of his clandestine acquisitions and he wasn't aware Reginald lived in New Manhattan and not near Blythe Space Port. The comm connected and Reggie heard the disembodied voice of the computer that ran *Mademoiselle Rouge,*

"I am yours to command."

"Altair, prepare the ship for liftoff. We'll be heading for the moon, but don't file a flight plane, yet. Understood?

"Gotcha, boss. We'll be ready in thirty minutes."

He disconnected and rose from his chair. Damn, he thought, I wonder what those ships are waiting for. Still, he was confident his forces could overcome any obstacle. He turned from the comm and left the room to prepare for his departure to the moon. What he didn't know was Joseph Warren had infiltrated his comm system and was fully aware of his plans. He, too, would be leaving for the moon shortly, and once there would confront Tebaldi and destroy him and his plans.

Tebaldi hailed a cab and headed for Teterboro space port. Once there he knew the trip to the moon would be quick. The Rouge was equipped with the latest Polson transluminal drive which included a state-of-the-art inertial suppression system. This allowed it to accelerate out of the Earth's gravity well and on to the moon at speeds that would allow it to arrive six hours after its departure.

It was a crisp autumn day and the sun shone without a cloud in the sky as the air cab began its descent into Teterboro. The cab slowed as it approached the landing pad adjacent to the private reception area and lazily turned to allow Reginald direct access to the entrance port.

"Welcome, Mr. Tebaldi. Do you have luggage?" The attendant said as Reggie alighted from the cab.

"No luggage, Stevens. I haven't logged a flight plan, yet. I'll send it once I'm aboard. I'll also need a shuttle to my ship."

"That was arranged when your ship's computer informed us of your trip."

Tebaldi had specifically requested this berth for its almost hidden location where very few people would notice his magnificent ship. *Mademoiselle Rouge* was a modern ship design with a highly polished deep red titanium-reinforced shell over a superstructure of plasteel. Her configuration was tapered. She was forty meters in length and twenty meters in width creating a teardrop appearance that belied her powerful engines and transluminal capability. Reginald had lavished a large amount of money both on the ship and its luxurious interior which could sleep six in complete comfort with a well-appointed galley, salon, and view lounge. The Rouge also had a fully operational landing bay in which Reginald stored a small runabout for those times he didn't want to expose the ship to prying eyes. For this trip, Reginald had also stored munitions and neutron bombs to be used by the force he was bringing to the moon.

"We've arrived, sir." the droid said as they pulled alongside Tebaldi's ship. He got out and walked over to the Mademoiselle Rouge.

"Access open," he said and immediately the airlock opened and Reggie stepped aboard. He climbed up the stairway which led to the salon and the bridge beyond that. As he was climbing, he started talking to the ship's computer.

"Altair, initiate the preflight system check and prepare for immediate departure. Set course for Tycho Base on Luna as programmed."

"Right, boss. Preflight operating. Liftoff in six minutes."

Reginald crossed the salon and entered the bridge just as the covers began to recede from the forward viewport. From this angle, he was looking back toward New Manhattan and the metropolis that seemed to float above the remains of the city that had preceded it. He quickly scanned the controls and seated himself at the main panel.

"Control, this is *Mademoiselle Rouge* preparing for departure."

"Traffic control here. You are second in line for departure and you will climb out to the east as you ascend. Your computer hasn't filed a flight plan. Before I give clearance, I must have your plan."

"Acknowledged, control. One moment."

"Altair, create a flight plan to take us to Delhi 1 and from there to Mars. Complete and file with control. Let me know the minute we're ready for departure."

"Thank you. Your plan is entered and set. You are free to depart. Have a safe trip *Mademoiselle Rouge*. Control out."

"Altair, once we clear the atmosphere reprogram to the instructions I am inputting now."

"Gotcha, boss".

Once clear Reginald planned to avoid the ships Nkosi had spoken of. Once he cleared the atmosphere, Barbarella would reset to the new flight plan. The new trajectory would take him longer to get to the moon but he felt it would be worth it. "Prepare for liftoff, boss man. T-minus thirty seconds." Altair intoned.

Reginald strapped himself into the gravity cushion and moments later he saw rather than felt a slight surge as the *Mademoiselle Rouge* started her ascent. The surface quickly receded and Reginald watched as New Manhattan became a very small gathering of buildings surrounded by water. Seven minutes after liftoff the Rouge entered its first orbit in preparation for the full circle which would take it out and away from Earth. The sky was spangled with stars and off to the left, Reginald could see Luna as a white sliver floating in the distance. He loosened his seatbelt and turned to the navigation panel. Everything was in order and the readout set an arrival time on the moon seven hours from now. Reginald was satisfied he would be able to enforce his will on the men and women living and working on the moon. After all, he had a force joining him that would take over Warren's forces when they arrived. Before that he wanted a little rest.

"Altair, wake me in three hours. We have a lot to accomplish before we reach Luna."

"Aye, mon Capitaine."

CHAPTER FIFTEEN

Joseph Warren was not one to allow people to usurp his control whatever the situation. He had known of Tebaldi's plans for more than a
month and was now preparing to lift off for the moon with the full
complement of mercenary security personnel that Reginald thought
were under his control. Warren had changed their orders and they were
now prepared to land at Tycho base. His orders were to assume full
control of the base, Luna City, and the mines. He also knew the residents would be unprepared for what was about to hit them. He arrived
at Blythe Space Port an hour before the scheduled departure. There
would be 100 ships lifting off within minutes of one another and as-
sembling to form an armada. He found the commander he had selected
to lead the first wave of the assault.

"Okay, Osgood, you'll be leading the first twelve ships to attack the
moon. You will push directly toward the moon and cross the embargo
three hours before the remaining force hits. I'll lead the rest of the armada and assume full command once we have assembled on the moon."

Warren then turned to his second in command, Randal Gupta.

"Once in orbit, the twelve ships under Osgood's command will separate from the main armada. The rest of the fleet will follow me. Do not
approach any of the platforms and make no contact with traffic control
either here or on the moon. Do you understand?"

"Yes, sir."

Warren was confident his team would gain the upper hand with the Lunatics and things would continue as before with Lunar Mines calling the shots.

Martin Kauri, aboard one of the new ships created by Lunar Freedom, was reviewing their preparations for the imminent attack. They were stationed at the Lagrange point between the Earth and the moon and would be the first to encounter the armada from the Earth.

"How is the set-up going?" he said to the science officer.

"We've created a web of invisible strands of tachyon pulses that will not only tell us when a ship enters the web but also will defuse and deactivate any lethal weapons that might be aboard."

"Once we've deactivated their weapons, also deactivate any type of propulsion system on the ships, slow them to a stop, and set them adrift. When we've disarmed their ships, we'll emit a counter agent beam across the tachyon grid."

It was just another of the many innovations Dr. Darwin had incorporated into the new ships he had created to protect the moon. What only Martin, Chuck Breckman, and Dr. Darwin knew was the existence of another ten ships exactly like the ten he had just deployed. He was holding them in reserve on the far side of the moon and they were waiting for his orders to join the fleet at the Lagrange point or any other location when needed.

Tebaldi and Warren were aware of the ten ships waiting between them and the moon and both believed they were more than capable of overwhelming the far smaller force. Martin was informed when Tebaldi's twelve ships departed Earth and it gave him enough time to prepare his team for their arrival at the Lagrange point. He had no intention of simply shooting them out of the void without any kind of warning. He would send a signal when they were still an hour away from his fleet.

Jason Escobar was in Moose Nkosi's office in Luna City at Tycho base. They were in the process of selecting the men and women who would be stationed at the various mine entrances and Luna City assembly points to protect Luna Mine's interests.

"I don't think it's a good idea to send me and my small team back to Aitken base. Send the commander from the incoming forces out to Aitken. My team is much better equipped to work with the population here. We know many of them and they'll listen to us."

"I'm not convinced but here's what I'll do. When the new team arrives, I'll interview the commander. If I believe he has what it takes to maintain control at Aitken I'll send his full complement of 1,800 men there and we'll keep the extra 20,000 here to control the population. For now, get in touch with Chuck Breckman and arrange a meeting. I want you to find out as much as you can about whatever plans Lunar Freedom has for its strike. Get going."

Jax's plans wouldn't work if he was sent to Aitken. He, Chuck, and Martin had formulated a scheme that would overturn the status quo and, at the same time, keep most of the citizens of the moon safe and ultimately in control of their destiny.

The ships carrying the 1,800 personnel from the Earth that Reginald

Tebaldi thought were under his control were approaching the blockade set up by Martin and the ten new ships he had created. They were unable to detect the tachyon grid created so were unaware the ships that were directly in front of their flight path would be able to impede them in any way. As they hurtled through the void, the captain of the lead ship contacted the remaining fleet.

"Captain Osgood to Luna Mines detachment, we are approaching the ships detected earlier on the moon and I am sending a warning to instruct them to retreat from their positions. Be prepared, however, for an attack or another type of diversion. Osgood out."

He turned to his first officer, directed him to maintain his course, and left the bridge for his ready room just off the conn.

Martin's ships had been tracking the approaching fleet and were now prepared to initiate the tachyon beams and at the same time warn the oncoming ships of the danger of trying to cross the blockade.

"Attention Lunar Mines ships approaching the embargo point for transit to the moon. Do not attempt to cross our lines. We have the ability to stop your progress and deactivate any large armaments you may have on board. Do not let our numbers influence your decision. We will stop any ship attempting to cross."

Martin purposely did not divulge his ability to compromise the attacking fleet's propulsion systems. He liked having a surprise up his sleeve.

He then turned to his comm operator and instructed her to send the prepared message he had created to Jax at Lunar City. In it, he told Jax the fleet had initiated the tachyon beams and were expecting an encounter with the LM ships within twenty minutes.

Jax had been in his office waiting for Martin's communication. Now it was up to him to secure Luna City and the Tycho base.

He turned to Andie Flannigan, who had been waiting with him,

"This is it, Andie. Get the team together and muster in the general recreation center. You, Rho, and Chan meet me in Moose's office right away and come armed. Hustle, we don't have very much time."

Andie rushed out of his office and Jax came around from his desk and headed for Nkosi's office. He hoped to catch him there alone and try to reason with him before he had to take more drastic action.

He knocked on Nkosi's door,

"Moose, it's Jax. May I have a word with you?"

"Come on in, kid. What can I do for you?"

Jax thought how much more difficult this was going to be than he had hoped. Moose had become a friend, of sorts since Jax's arrival on the moon and Jax didn't want to hurt him if he didn't have to. He came in and sat down across the desk from Moose.

"It seems the first deployment of mercenaries is approaching the LaGrange point. They won't be allowed to cross. Martin is in command of the ten ships that were here the other day and he is prepared to stop them from entering Luna space."

"What the hell are you talking about? How do you get your information?"

"I have been part of the uprising for the past few months and I intend to help Lunar Freedom and the citizens of Luna gain their independence from Lunar Mines and its harsh control of the lives of everyone living on this satellite."

"You're out of your mind, Escobar. The backup fleet will kill everyone connected to this ersatz rebellion. They're equipped with weapons that can kill everyone on the moon if needed."

"Moose, what good would that do either for Lunar Mines or the moon? It's time the Lunatics controlled their own lives and Lunar

Mines needs to be held accountable for the injustices that have been going on since they first established a small operation at Tycho base. Don't fight us, join us."

"I'm sorry, Escobar, but that's something I can't do," Moose said as he rose from his chair and pointed a lasgun at Jax.

"Get up. You're going to the brig right now." He waved the lasgun in the general direction of the door and started to step around and push Jax toward the opening.

The door suddenly opened and three of Jax's team, led by Isabell Rho, came in with guns drawn, as well.

"Don't even think about it, Nkosi. There are another fifteen of us outside and you won't make it three meters down the hall before we either kill you or take you prisoner. Now, drop the gun and slowly turn around with your hands above your head."

Nkosi did as he was told and within moments his wrists were bound and Rho began to walk him out the door and to the brig.

"You can't get away with this, Escobar. The larger force will annihilate you and everyone associated with this ill-thought scheme. Warren and Tebaldi won't let this stand."

Jax ignored the comments as Moose was walked out the door. He quickly returned to Moose's desk and picked up the comm.

"Attention security personnel. This is Escobar. Nkosi is no longer in charge of the security on the moon and I have been put in charge. All personnel report to Tycho base headquarters immediately. This order rescinds all other orders. This is not a drill."

He put the comm down and left Nkosi's office. Andie was waiting outside and looked at him with concern.

"What's up, boss?"

"The insurrection has begun, Flannigan. Our core team is now in charge of all security on the moon. When Rho finishes with Nkosi, get together with her and Chan and organize the rest of our team for action. Once the remainder of the security force is gathered at Tycho base give them an ultimatum. Work with us or spend the next few days in the brig. Send the same message to Aitken at the same time. Take the maglev between here and there out of service so we'll know exactly where that team is at all times."

"Got it, Jax. You know we've got your back," she said as she turned and started toward the magtube to Tycho Base.

So, it has begun. All Jax had to do now was wait for Martin's comm as to the action in space. If Lunar Mines tried to pass the ships through his blockade there would be confusion for the invaders. They would be unable to counter Martin's beam at first and be at a loss as to what to do. But, how long would it take them to devise some sort of defense? Jax knew this was just the beginning of a more drawn-out confrontation.

CHAPTER SIXTEEN

Captain Osgood's training was in security and crowd control. He had been assigned to lead the first wave of security personnel simply because he was in command of the first ship of the twelve selected to lead the attack. He had never been in any confrontation and he was nervous. As they approached the blockade he returned to the bridge and turned to his second in command.

"Okay, Wilson, tighten up the other ships. I want all twelve of our ships to cross together between the ships that are out there waiting for us. Space everyone to slide past at the same time following this lead ship. Move us slightly forward of the advancing fleet. I'll show them what trained and disciplined personnel knows how to do when confronted by insurgents."

Wilson began sending out instructions to the other ships and letting the commanders on those ships know when they expected to meet the Lunatics.

"Wilson to all ships. We will be passing through the blockade, such as it is, in six minutes. We'll warn the insurgents to stay clear of our ships and remain where they are. Wilson out."

"Mr. Osgood, we're in position and will pass through the blockade in less than three minutes."

"Very good, Wilson."

Osgood turned to his comm and once again sent a message to the

Lunatics.

"This is Osgood of the Lunar Mines security forces. We will be passing through your area shortly. Do not attempt to approach any of our ships. If you do, you will be blown into space dust. Osgood out."

The reply from Martin was almost instantaneous.

"We warn you again, Mr. Osgood, not to cross our perimeter. We will destroy any ship that tries to pass between us and the moon. Turn back at once."

"Mr. Wilson, continue this course. I have no intention of letting them use a bluff to try to stop us. Once we are beyond the perimeter continue to Tycho base and Luna City."

The ships continued to hurtle toward the blockade. As they got closer Martin continued to send messages to try to stop their progress but to no avail.

The Lunar Mines ships were within twenty seconds of passing the blockade and Martin knew they were doomed.

Osgood, whose ship was slightly ahead of the others, hit the tachyon screen first.

There was no immediate reaction and the ships continued as before for about 10 seconds. Then the ships began to separate and lose attitude control. They ceased to move as a unit and began to slow to a stop. They were quickly adrift with no means of propulsion.

"Well, that cuts it," Martin said.

"I tried to tell them but they wouldn't listen. There are an additional eighty-eight ships on the way. I'm sending them a comm showing what happened to the first twelve. I'm also sending the same comm to Escobar at Tycho base. Ladies and gentlemen, from this point on we are at war with Lunar Mines and possibly all of the Earth."

Jax and Andie watched the vid Martin sent down and Jax was happy his team had been able to stop the fleet and the possible carnage. He hoped the next wave of ships would return to Earth without trying again.

"I suppose it's going to be a full-fledged war before we can pull away from Lunar Mines and control from Earth. For now, however, we need to get complete control of the forces here on Luna. How are we getting along with bringing the rest of the security teams in from the other mines and outposts?" Jax asked.

"We have a total of 141 personnel on the moon working for LM as security forces. As you know Rho, Chan, and I have been working to ensure most of the team is on board with us for this takeover. There will be a few holdouts but I believe we have at least 120 who are loyal to us and the Lunatics and want to continue living on the moon. If that second wave breaks through, we'll have a fight on our hands but I believe we can keep the secure areas in our control. The one thing we don't know is what kinds of weapons they will bring."

"Don't worry about what kinds of weapons as much as how adept they will be on the moon. Most of them will never have set foot here and at first, won't know how to control themselves. We'll have an advantage along with the innovative weapon Dr. Darwin has installed in the new ships. This comm changes the way we'll protect our home and ensure we are allowed to live the way we want to."

"I'll let you know as soon as the whole security team is at Tycho base," Andie said as she walked out the door.

Jax sat for a moment looking at the comm screen which held a still photo of the forces from Earth drifting in space. More ships were coming and he hoped the vid Martin had sent those ships would stop them or at least slow them down. Now was the time for Jax to get in touch with Chuck. He and Lunar Freedom members would have to help on the front lines if it came to that. Organizing that group into a disciplined and effective fighting team would take some work and they needed to start right now.

The miners, citizens, and business owners had, for some time, been aware of the impending confrontation. Most, if not all, were willing to stand with the security team Jax had created to protect their property and their homes. It would be these citizen fighters that would help Jax and his team use the resources Martin had put together to defend themselves should the forces of Joseph Warren reach the moon. Jax was in Nkosi's central command office and he reached for the comm.

"This is security central, Jason Escobar commanding. Attention all residents of Luna. The first wave of Lunar Mines forces has been stopped at the Lagrange point between the Earth and Luna. They no longer pose a threat to our homes. A second much larger force is still on the way. For those citizens living at Aitken mine, stay where you are. A security team will join you shortly with weapons and instructions on their use and how to defend yourselves. Lunar Freedom members will assist the security team with the distribution of the weapons and training."

Jax continued,

"To the residents of Luna City, assemble at the central dome to receive weapons and training. You will then return to your home districts and await further orders. Each of you knows what must be done and the most important thing to remember is to keep calm. I believe we'll stop any attempt to land on Luna with the forces we have in place to protect the moon. As I told you, we were successful in destroying the first wave of the attack and we will prevail when the second wave tries to enter our space. Escobar out."

The plans he, Martin, and Breckman had formulated over the past twelve months would now be put into place. Breckman had worked with Lunar Freedom members to create a de facto militia that would lead the rest of the citizens should the need arise. Martin, for his part, had imported weapons from the Earth and stored them both at Aitken mine and in Luna City. These would now be dispersed to the Lunar Freedom fighters and those citizens who had joined the resistance. Jax would lead the overall attempt to secure the moon for everyone and act as a spokesman when, hopefully, there came a time to negotiate with Lunar Mines. Everything was in place and now they would wait for the showdown.

Joseph Warren was surprised when he received the vid of the drifting remains of his scout patrol. That surprise quickly turned to anger as he watched the vid again and again.

"What gives this rabble the right to stop my forces? Don't they know Lunar Mines is the legal owner of the mines?"

He was on the bridge of his command ship and turned to his second in command, who had been trained for combat and assault operations before joining Lunar Mines. As a mercenary, he had completed more than twenty clandestine missions all around the solar system for LM. He was ruthless in his ambition and hungry for the fight ahead.

"What are your plans, Smith?"

"For the moment we can't cross that embargo line. I want to leave the ecliptic, ascend up and over the line then come blazing down on those Lunatics. They'll know we've gone over them but there's not a lot they can do once we make our move. We'll be coming at them from a completely different angle than they'll expect."

"You've got eighty-eight remaining ships. I'll transfer to one of the rear guards and remain there with a total of twelve ships. Once you've broken their line, I'll join the force for the final assault on Luna City and Tycho Base. From there we can go to Aitken and overcome any type of resistance there might be." Warren turned and left the bridge. He would take a small runabout and join the twelve ships he intended to hold back from the new plan.

Martin Kauri kept his ships in position and watched as the second wave continued to approach the moon. His second in command, Nancy Strong, was at the helm and waited as Martin thought over his options.

"What do you think, Strong, will they stop?"

"Hard to tell, sir. They haven't slowed down and will hit our barrier within three hours if they don't change course. A funny thing, though, twelve ships have dropped back from the rest. I don't know what it means but we'll keep tabs on them, as well."

"I'll be in my ready room. Have the comm keep a close watch on the ships and let me know if there's any change, at all, in their trajectory."

He wasn't taking any chances and went to his ready room to contact the second ten ships in orbit on the far side of the moon.

"Kauri to Dr. Darwin. Come in, please. Kauri to Dr. Darwin."

"Martin, I just saw the results of your encounter with the lead ships. They didn't believe we could stop them, did they?"

"No, Doctor, they didn't. The second wave is still on course to intercept our embargo point within three hours. I want you to remain on stand-by in case I need you in a hurry. It seems twelve of the ships have split off from the others and are slowing their approach. I don't know what they're planning but we'll keep watching until they make a move. Kauri out."

CHAPTER SEVENTEEN

Joseph Warren stayed behind with the twelve ships he had separated from the remaining fleet.

"Okay, helm. The seventy-six ships under Nahral Smith's command will continue on the original course. He won't make his move until he's within ten minutes of the blockade. Once there the whole compliment would change course and hurtle at a ninety-degree angle away from the orbit of the Earth and moon."

"Aye, sir. When that happens what do you want us to do?"

"None of these ships is particularly fast but my plan anticipates the unexpected change will catch the Lunatics off guard."

Warren decided not to share with the helm that once they were away from the blockade, Smith planned to turn sharply back toward the moon and come at them with the sun behind his fleet. He was sure Luna City and Tycho Base would be unable to stop them before it was too late.

Martin Kauri waited on the bridge of his command vessel. He and his officers were watching the maneuvers of the seventy-six ships still approaching at a high speed. He continued to send out the warning to stay clear but the ships wouldn't stop. They were now within a few minutes of hitting the blockade.

"Okay, Nancy, get ready for the impact of those ships hitting the tachyon screen. I've tried everything I know to stop them."

Suddenly, the lead ship turned sharply away from the blockade followed immediately by the remaining ships.

"What the—. Where are they going? Alright Strong, tell me what's happening."

"They are escaping above the ecliptic and seem to be accelerating. The remaining twelve ships have slowed to a stop."

"This is Kauri to all ships. Retreat to an orbit fifteen hundred kilometers above the moon. Second tier, join us above the moon in the configuration planned for a frontal attack. Use emergency thrust, they'll be coming at us from outside the ecliptic and we don't have much time. Kauri out."

"Nancy, move us into position at the fastest possible speed to take our place in the new blockade. Hurry."

Martin watched as his small assembly of ships began their maneuvers and scattered to regroup just above the moon. This is going to be close, he thought, as he hurried to warn the surface of what was about to happen.

"Escobar, come in, this is Kauri."

"Escobar here. What's happening, Martin?"

"The approaching vessels have jumped above the ecliptic and I believe they plan to attack from outside our orbit. I've moved all twenty ships to within fifteen hundred kilometers above the moon. We're going to create a tighter screen that should be able to move quickly enough to block an attack from whatever quadrant they choose. If they all hit at once, however, our ships and even the surface might be impacted by the blasts if they fire any type of weapon before hitting the grid. Get everyone into the deepest underground shafts at the mines. Clear Luna City as quickly as possible. We don't have much time."

"Roger that. Take care of yourself, Martin; I want you back here on the moon."

"Don't worry, Jax, I know what I'm doing. I want to return to the moon, as well. Kauri, out."

"Wake up, boss. There's action out there and you might want to see what's happening." Altair said.

Reginald Tebaldi hurried to the bridge and watched as the unexpected fleet from Blythe Space Port hurried to the moon. It wasn't what he had planned and understood now that Warren had double-crossed him. It was obvious he knew of his plans and wouldn't be interested in anything he would have to say.

As he watched, a smaller flight of twelve ships separated from the main fleet and accelerated toward the moon. Tebaldi knew of the blockade but had not been monitoring the comm so didn't know of the warnings being sent out to the approaching vessels. As the ships approached the blockade, he thought they might slow, but they continued to the point Tebaldi knew was the blockade and then he watched as all twelve ships slowed to a stop and began to drift.

"What was that, Allie ? What happened?"

"There was some sort of filter or screen across the space they tried to traverse. Something deactivated the propulsion on the ships."

Tebaldi knew he needed to get closer to the moon without attracting attention to his ship. He also didn't want to take a chance with the bombs he had in his hold.

"Altair, reset the course. Let's get around to the backside of the moon as quickly as possible. I don't know what's going to happen but we need to be closer to the action. Keep us one thousand kilometers above the moon. Do it now." ."

He knew there just might be a chance for him if he could get to the surface of the moon first. He would get to Escobar and take control of the situation and lead the force that would destroy Warren and his mercenaries. From there he would take over Lunar Mines.

"Okay, Nancy," Martin said. "What's taking so long? We need all twenty-four ships in position to protect Tycho Base and Luna City. I'm going to spread our forces across a far wider expanse than previously planned. If we don't get closer together those Lunar Mines forces will be able to flank our ships unless we're separated too far apart."

He decided to create a net that would spread over more than forty percent of the moon's surface which faces the Earth. His main focus now was to protect Luna City and Tycho base from the invaders. The comm continued to track the ships that had left the plane of the ecliptic and kept sending data to the navigation chief.

"Nancy, we need to be in position before they come our way again."

"The final positions have been plotted and we'll be ready for them in two minutes. We're spread pretty thin and some of the ships might get through."

"Start the tachyon emissions as soon as you're ready. Move it."

Martin stepped to the comm and saw his small fleet was now ready for the attackers.

The seventy-six Lunar Mines ships under the command of Nahral Smith aboard the *Rings of Saturn* were still heading out of the solar system and now was the time to turn back toward the moon.

"Helm, don't slow down but take us back to the moon at the fastest possible speed. Don't brake until the last minute. I want to surprise them, if possible, and catch them before they can prepare a defense."

The helmsman now took the *Rings of Saturn*, Smith's lead ship, and started a large sweeping turn to head back toward the moon. He looked nervously at Smith and then back to his screen.

"Don't worry, son. With hard braking, we'll end up hovering just above the surface when we come to a stop. Don't think about the first wave that we left drifting in space. They'll be alright and will join us once we've taken the moon. I have no fear of the screen those Lunatics set up for the first attack and I'm confident we will prevail."

Jax and Andie were still in Nkosi's headquarters and continued to get comm messages from personnel throughout Luna City, Tycho base, and the Aitken mine.

"Aitken mine to Escobar. We are fully prepared and our team has armed the civilian population. We've also moved all non-essential personnel to the deepest areas of the mines. Aitken base out."

"Chuck Breckman, here. Old Town is ready, Jax. Everyone is prepared for what may come. Citizens not part of the Lunar Freedom militia have been issued small arms and instructed to seek shelter in the deepest parts of the city, base, and mine."

"John Breckman with Lunar Freedom at the Luna City. We've armed eight hundred Lunar Freedom members with heavier weapons and they've now gathered under the dome in Luna City."

Thanks, John. Flannigan and I will join your team as soon as we know what form the next attack would take. Escobar out."

Nahral Smith, aboard the *Rings of Saturn*, turned to his helmswoman and gave her instructions to continue on the course set for the moon.

"Once on the surface, I plan to enter Luna City and take immediate control of the security center. Once established we'll hold the city and move to Tycho Base and Aitken mine to round up the last of what must be a small group of disgruntled employees."

He already saw himself standing before Joseph Warren as the victor of the attack that was about to begin.

Mademoiselle Rouge was approaching the moon from the far side and Reginald was deep in thought. He certainly didn't want to expose himself to any sort of danger but things were moving now at such a swift pace he might find that hard to achieve. Suddenly Barbarella's voice broke his reverie.

"Hey, boss, there's something you need to see. It looks like ten ships coming in from the dark side. Their configuration matches the ten Lunatic ships we saw earlier. They've just started to brake and I project they will come in just under us. I have stopped our descent and will hold until further instructions."

"Good work, Al. Do you think they've seen us?"

"I can't tell, boss. They haven't deviated from their course and I believe we just aren't on their screens. The larger attacking force has also changed course and is now headed right for the blockade. They should cross it in two minutes."

"Great, let's just hold here for a while and see what happens."

So, Tebaldi thought, a smaller group of ships was coming in from behind. He intended to wait until the larger force hit the blockade and either made it through or was stopped like the others. What happened there would give him the information he needed to begin his assault on the moon and its inhabitants.

Joseph Warren watched from his safe position as the fleet he had sent ahead hurtled toward the moon's surface.

"Sir," the helm said. "They will reach the blockade within two minutes. What is your command?"

Warren wasn't at all sure they would prevail. The movement of the Luna ships to hover closer to the surface and the sudden appearance of ten more ships gave him an uneasy feeling and he thought he was right to save himself for the fight to come. There was no thought, at all, for the men and women on the moon who were in danger or of the people forced to attack the lunar compounds. The moon was his and he intended to take it whatever the cost.

CHAPTER EIGHTEEN

The larger fleet, hurtling toward the moon, believed they would be able to break through the net set up by Martin and his new ships because of the size and speed of the armada he led.

"Helm, can't you take us faster? I want to completely surprise that rebel trash. Increase speed."

"Sir, we're approaching twenty-five percent luminal as it is. We still need to be able to stop after we've broken through the blockade."

"I didn't ask for your opinion, helm. Increase speed. That is a direct order."

The helm responded by increasing their dive speed to five percent luminal. They began to pull away from the rest of the fleet which had not increased speed because there had been no order to do so. Those commanders were well aware of the time and space it would take to reduce speed after passing through the blockade.

"Sir, we should pass through the blockade in six seconds."

"Don't slow down, helm, until every ship is through."

As the leader passed through the blockade the helm attempted to begin the braking maneuver even though it contradicted the captain.

"Sir, sir," a horrified helm began to scream.

"Nothing is happening. I can't stop."

On his own ship, Warren watched as the lead ship, captained by Nahral Smith, continued its headlong rush to the surface of the moon.

"What was he thinking?" Warren said out loud to no one in particular.

The ships that were following the *Rings of Saturn* were disabled but because of their slower speed, most were able to engage the braking maneuver before all controls were disabled. Not so with the leader.

"Stop us helm, stop us!" Smith screamed as his ship headed for total destruction.

The *Rings of Saturn* impacted the lunar regolith, and the explosion was blinding and the power of the vessel created a new impact crater for the moon. Many of the following ships were caught in the outward exploding debris but managed to maintain the integrity of their hulls. Nahral Smith's dream of complete subjugation of the moon had ended and with it any chance that Joseph Warren might be able to simply take over the moon.

Martin, from his ship, and Jax, with his team in the command center, watched as the massive destroyer was obliterated.

"Martin, what happened? I thought all the ships would simply be disabled."

"It was the speed of the lead ship, Jax. They were going too fast once they passed through the tachyon field for our beam to control stopping them like the other ships. The commander made a very serious error in judgment. The other ships were disabled by our beams and we were able to stop all forward momentum."

"Joseph Warren is going to blame us, you know. We've disabled eighty-eight of his ships. I'm sure I'll hear from him shortly. I'll get Chuck up to speed and let him negotiate with Warren. I'm going to send a team out to the wreckage even though I know there is no hope of finding survivors."

"Okay, Jax. I'm taking half the fleet over to Tycho Base and sending the other half into hiding. We'll await your orders. Kauri out."

Next, Jax called Chuck on his comm.

"You saw? That ship could carry more than two hundred people. They were out of control."

"Yeh," Chuck responded. "It's a tragedy that could have been avoided had they heeded our warnings."

"Warren is still sitting out there and I don't know what he has in mind. What I do know is he will have to contact us, now. I'm no diplomat, Chuck, I think you're the man to deal with Joseph Warren when he makes contact. You have a better sense of what we want and how to deal with Lunar Mines and the Lunar Management Company. Can you do that?"

"Of course, I can, but I also want to convene a meeting of the leadership of Lunar Freedom. Together we can come up with a plan to ensure Warren can't arrive and somehow gain the upper hand. I'll get back to you once we have a plan in place."

"Altair, what happened?" Tebaldi asked the computer.

"The lead ship was traveling at a velocity that exceeded its ability to slow enough to prevent hitting the surface. The yield was the force of three hundred megatons and created a new impact crater more than twenty kilometers across. The debris that wasn't thrown into space will settle to the surface over the next twenty-four hours."

"What's happening with the rebel fleet? Where are they now?"

"The twenty ships are beginning to disperse and are already headed away from this area. Ten have set a course that will take them to Tycho Base. The other ten are heading to the far side of the moon."

"What's happening with the twelve ships Warren held back?"

"Nothing, mon Capitaine. They have remained unmoved since backing off from the main fleet."

"Good, get us over to Tycho Base before the rebels realize we're here. Move it" "Aye, boss."

Reginald Tebaldi intended to arrive at Tycho Base before the rebels or Warren could make a move. He would meet with Nkosi and give him his instructions. He would be in command of the situation within an hour of touching down. Ah, he thought, I couldn't have planned it better myself. The *Mademoiselle Rouge* had already accelerated out of low orbit and was rushing toward Tycho Base.

"What the hell happened, helm?" Warren almost screamed.

"Sir, Commander Smith took his ship in too fast. Once it was disabled by whatever this new weapon is he was unable to control his ship and it impacted the moon."

"I saw that myself, I want to know how it happened," Smith shouted.

The woman at the helm was unable to answer and Joseph Warren turned from the comm in a rage. How could an unarmed group of roughnecks and scum defeat his fleet and his well-thought-out plan? What to do now? He had twelve ships with a complement of 2400 mercenaries who were very capable of taking over Tycho Base once they were on the surface. But the question was how to get them on the surface? He quickly realized he would have to talk to the rabble on the moon and persuade them to allow his ships to land. He wouldn't tell them about the soldiers he had on board and he would instruct their leader to keep them there until he had talked with the insurrectionist. He would pretend there was only a modest security team on the ships and they were no threat to the Lunatics.

CHAPTER NINETEEN

Mademoiselle Rouge would be over Tycho Base within twenty minutes and Tebaldi still hadn't decided exactly how he would gain access to the base and ultimately gain control of Luna City and the moon.

"Altair, contact control at Tycho Base and tell them I want to talk to Jason Escobar. At the same time, access landing coordinates and announce arrival for an immediate touchdown."

"I'm on it, my commander."

As a plan began to form, Reginald decided to pretend he had no idea of the larger force that had been sent to attack the moon. He would claim he had come to help the Lunatics and protect the interests of Luna Mines and the residents of Luna. Would Escobar believe him? He would find out very soon.

"Captain, Tycho Base on Comm 2, Jason Escobar."

"Okay, Al, patch me in."

He turned to the comm screen over the control panel and saw Jason Escobar in the frame.

"What do you want, Tebaldi? You are not welcome here and I would suggest you return to Earth."

"Jax, Jax, don't be that way. I didn't know about the attack Joseph Warren had planned for Luna. I came here to help you and the Lunatics. Trust me, I had no idea."

"It's too convenient for you to show up just as we gain the upper hand with the attackers. As I remember from the Earth, you took orders only from Warren. Try again."

"Okay, I did put a small team together which I instructed to take over Tycho Base but I never planned to go farther than protect the mines and get them working again. Warren somehow became aware of what I had planned and took over my small group of ships and combined them with his. Those were the ships you somehow stopped from being able to attack the base. It was the lead ship that you destroyed although Warren wasn't aboard. I believe he is with the remaining 12 ships waiting at the LaGrange point."

"I still don't believe you, Tebaldi. You work much too closely with Warren not to have known of his complete plans."

"Not so, Jax. For more than five years I've been secretly working to distance myself from Warren and one day overthrow his control of the LMC Security Council. I plan to put myself in that place and move Luna Mines into a more productive corporation and one that will give back to the workers some of the profit we enjoy."

"That sounds a little more like it. I don't believe you want to help the miners but I certainly see you would work to destroy Warren. Is your ship armed?"

"I dumped all ordinances before coming over the horizon. May I land?"

"I'll hand you over to control and they will give your computer coordinates for one of the landing pads. There'll be an armed guard waiting for you and they'll bring you directly to control. Don't lock out access to your ship, we want to search it. There are still a lot of unanswered questions and I want to know more about the remaining ships Warren has out there. Tycho Base out."

Jax turned to Screed and issued the commands necessary to bring

Tebaldi directly to control.

"Rho and Chan, come in," Jax said as he turned to the central comm.

"Rho here, sir, and Chan is next to me."

"Good. A ship, the *Mademoiselle Rouge*, will be landing shortly and the pilot will be brought here under armed guard. I want you two to take a team and search the ship. Be careful, there may be some sort of trap or computer command that might be lethal. Let me know what you find as quickly as possible."

Once he had Tebaldi in custody and knew his ship was unarmed or had been unarmed by his team, he would talk with the man who seemed to want to take control. Would he be interested or able to negotiate with Chuck Breckman as the new leader of Luna Freedom?

Joseph Warren was in no mood to simply sit and wait until all options were gone.

"Helm, move us to within ten thousand kilometers of the surface. Let me know when we're in position."

"Aye, sir," helm responded.

"Estimated time of arrival is three hours."

Once on the moon, Warren would be able to get a plan into motion that would allow his whole team to touch down and overwhelm the Lunatics. He would pretend his twelve ships held only a few dozen security personnel. The rest would be hidden in the cargo bays and would wait until Warren had taken control of the command center. He didn't know if he would be allowed a personal vibragun so there had to be another way to arrive armed. Better yet, he would set up a series of powerful laser guns in the cargo bays which could be brought against

Tyco Base control once he had taken the command center. He decided to secrete a small sonic pulse weapon that could easily be hidden on his person. It was a lethal weapon in close quarters and with the luck of surprise, he would kill them where they stood, and before they had a chance to warn anyone.

"Jax, come in Jax," Martin said into his comm.

"Jax here, Martin. Go ahead."

"I'm separating this group of ten. Five will go into reserve behind the moon and the other five I'll send to Aitken mine and set up a smaller screen. I don't want to get caught by a flanking maneuver."

"Good call, Martin. Jax out."

"Chuck Breckman report to command center."

When he arrived Jax had a little surprise for him.

"Chuck, Reginald Tebaldi decided to drop in. I don't trust him but have allowed him to land. I am taking him into armed custody and searching his ship. He says he has nothing to do with Warren's fleet of ships and came out here to help us out if he can. What do you think?"

"Taking him into custody is the best plan and searching his ship should give us a better idea of what he wants. Keep him locked up until we meet with Warren."

"That's what I had planned. Warren's ships have started moving this way but they won't arrive for another three hours. How are you coming with a set of demands?"

"We've decided to declare the moon a new independent world. We've drafted a letter of intent to send to the Lunar Management Company stating we are no longer a member of that organization until our freedoms are recognized by them and we are named an independent world. Once we all agree on the language, I am going to send the same declaration to all the outposts in the solar system. I expect we will receive overwhelming support from every colony."

"Good work, Chuck. Have the declaration ready in two hours. I expect Joseph Warren will not be a man who'll wait around while we decide what we want to do now that we've created Lunar Freedom."

"I'm on it. Thanks, Jax."

Within three hours Jax would have both Joseph Warren and Reginald Tebaldi in his control.

"Flannigan and Cho, report to Control. Escobar out."

"What's going on, boss?" Flannigan said as they entered.

"Place undercover armed guards here in the command center and along the corridors between Tycho Base and Luna City. We want to protect the assets of this satellite as well as the lunatics at all costs. Instruct them to be aware of potential threats in the way of planted bombs or other munitions. That's all. Get on it, pronto."

Now, all he had to do was await the touchdown of the ships that held Reginald Tebaldi and Joseph Warren.

CHAPTER TWENTY

Mademoiselle Rouge settled onto the designated landing pad with a spray of dust, small stones, and the debris that is always on the surface of the moon. Jax had instructed the landing officer not to extend the umbilicus to the ship. Rho, Chan, and a team of ten security personnel hurried to the vessel even before the dust settled. They were armed and were taking no chances of being caught off guard should Tebaldi attempt to leave his ship or in any way try to attack the team or the base. Once the team was in place Jax went to the comm and contacted Tebaldi.

"Okay, Tebaldi, you'll exit your ship and be taken into custody by the security personnel waiting for you. Do not attempt to flee, I have a mega-pulse weapon aimed at your propulsion systems and I won't hesitate to fire. Take it nice and slow when you step out with your hands above your head. Do you understand?"

"Jax, Jax, don't treat me this way. I'm here to help you secure a better future for the moon and the Lunatics."

"Don't even try, Tebaldi. Get suited up and out of your ship in ten minutes or I'll be forced to destroy it and you with it. Do it now. Escobar out."

Jax turned to Breckman,

"How am I doing, Chuck? Do you think he's going to make trouble?"

"We'll wait and see. I don't think he'll try anything right now. Be careful when your team goes into the ship. He probably wouldn't destroy it but he might have some nasty surprises for your security team. What we need to work on are your diplomatic skills." Chuck added with a smirk.

Nine minutes later the outer hatch of the *Mademoiselle Rouge* opened and Tebaldi stepped from his ship in a bright red surface suit. He was immediately restrained with his arms behind his back and led away to the landing center and from there to a holding cell within Tycho Base. Security went to the hatch and began to scan for any weapons or any type of booby trap Tebaldi might have planted before leaving. They entered and began a complete search of the ship. Once inside they removed their helmets but remained alert for any change in pressure.

"Computer, allow access," Rho said.

Nothing happened and she called for her weapons tech.

"Hanson, see if you can get anything out of the command computer. I don't care if you have to rough it up but get it operational for us. I want to see where he's been and where he might have plans to go. Give me a shout if you get anything."

Rho had assigned Chan the task of searching the cargo and landing bay and wasn't surprised when Chan called on the comm.

"We've found a cache of bombs and other ordinance. I'm in the process of disarming the whole bunch and should be finished within ten minutes. Chan out."

"Hanson here, ma'am. I've been able to open the computer but it's been a tough nut to crack. It was programmed to lift off if we tried to access it but I was able to take away its upper-level cognitive functions before it initiated its programming. He left Earth and has been circling the moon while Warren's forces were coming this way. The only other setting was a course for Mars. You might also be interested to know Tebaldi was planning on attacking with Warren's forces when they arrived. The computer is harmless, now. Hanson out."

Rho immediately transferred that information to Jax in the command center.

"Okay, Rho. Tebaldi is already in a holding cell and I'll begin an interview now that we know the ship isn't some sort of Trojan horse. Thanks. Get your team back inside as quickly as possible."

Jax left the command center and made his way to the cell in which Tebaldi was held. He entered and walked up to the barred wall. Tebaldi was dressed in a bright red tight-fitting jumpsuit. He looked as if he had no care in the world but stood up when Jax approached the cell. Before he could speak Jax said,

"I let you land only because I want to know at all times where you are and what you're doing. Don't for a minute think you can talk your way out of this."

"What makes you think I don't have information that might be vital to you and the Freedom Lunar movement?"

"Is that a tease or do you have pertinent information?" Jax said.

"I want to be released before we continue. I know the strength of Warren's assault team and how he's going to use them. Let me out."

"No, I don't think so. We've already incapacitated the whole fleet except for twelve ships approaching from the Earth. They were part of the original 100 he started with. At this point, I think we know what to expect. Anything you might add won't change what's going to happen." Jax turned away and spoke to the guards.

"Keep him in here until I order otherwise. Do not, under any circumstances, allow him visitors or any outside contact. Do you understand?"

"Yes, sir. He won't see anyone or speak to anyone."

Jax headed back to the command center. Tebaldi was unable to offer anything Lunar Freedom didn't already know. Still, he didn't trust him and aimed to keep him locked up until this whole thing was over. Even then Jax knew he would continue to be a threat to the freedom of the Lunatics and possibly the rest of the solar system. Jax would let Chuck Breckman handle him once the encounter with Joseph Warren and his ships was over. Assuming, of course, Lunar Freedom prevailed.

Joseph Warren was standing on the bridge of his ship in what could only be called an apoplectic fit. He had just read the demands the inhabitants of the moon released to LMC, the Earth, and all the colonized planets in the solar system and beyond. His rage at the Lunatics held no bounds and he was determined to retake the moon for LMC and, of course, himself.

"Comm, get me that son of a bitch Escobar now!"

He paced the bridge as he waited for the comm to respond. Who did they think they were? Declaring themselves an independent world? He had no intention of letting that happen.

"Sir. Jason Escobar is on comm 3."

"Escobar, who the hell do you think you are? There is no way LMC, or the Earth for that matter, will recognize your absurd declaration. The moon is owned by LMC and I will see to it I protect the assets of the company. Stand down from this insane movement. I will be Lunaside within two hours with enough men and women to take control of the satellite."

"Listen, Warren, you won't be allowed to land. Our forces stopped all your other ships and it will stop yours. Why don't you return to Earth and find a way to work with us? As an independent world, we plan to federate with the other outposts. Many have already confirmed their support. You can't succeed."

"Be that as it may, I will be Lunaside soon. When I arrive, I will take over and throw anyone in the brig who refuses to lay down their arms. Warren out."

Jax didn't reply and turned to his comm officer.

"Contact Flannigan, Kauri, and the squad commanders. We'll be ready for whatever Warren has up his sleeve."

As Jax waited for the comms to connect he thought about his options. They had the weapon needed to stop Warren but would he acquiesce? Should he allow Warren to land? If so, would he be able to neutralize any force he might have with him?

"Sir, the team is ready."

"Warren has declared he will be Lunaside within two hours. I don't' know what his plans might be but we must be ready. Flannigan, meet with the squad leaders and beef up security in and around the landing pads. Martin, make sure the screen is secure over Luna City. Also, prepare the additional ships for battle at a moment's notice. Okay, everyone, none of us knows exactly what to expect so stay on your toes. Escobar out."

Joseph Warren was aware his ship would never get through whatever had stopped the other ships. He could, he realized, use a much smaller runabout and sneak under the screen by coming in from the north pole of the moon.

"Helm, stay on course. Bring the ship to 80,000 kilometers above the satellite and hold. I'm leaving on the runabout with a small team to get on the surface. Once in place, I'll deactivate the ships blocking access to the surface and then you can land and commence the takeover."

Warren left the bridge and went to his ready room. Once there he went to his computer and entered a series of programs. He closed the connection, looked around the room, and headed for the cargo bay. He would meet his team there and they would head for the surface.

Jax and his team watched as Warren's ship slowed to a stop 80,000 meters above the surface. Scans revealed a small runabout leaving the ship and heading for the far side of the moon. Jax informed Andie and the other squad leaders and they continued to watch the immobile ship above them. Suddenly, the ship began to move toward the moon. It accelerated at an amazing speed and within moments was bearing down on Luna City.

"Comm, to all stations. Prepare for impact. Seal all pressure doors and move as quickly as possible to deeper areas of the settlement. Now!" Then, he commed Martin.

"Martin, Warren's ship is heading for Luna City. Can you stop it?"

"We saw him start to move. He's still accelerating. We're calculating the precise point of impact. Don't worry, we'll either stop him or push him off course."

For more than a minute they were all mesmerized as the ship continued to increase speed and come closer and closer to the moon's surface.

"Sir, the ship will strike in less than 30 seconds."

"Thanks, comm, let's see what Kauri can do," Jax responded.

The ship was less than 800 Kilometers above the surface when it veered toward the small mountain range to the east of Luna City. The solar farm was in that direction and it appeared Warren wanted to destroy the moon's main power source. The area itself was a very sparsely populated area that had been evacuated when the trouble started. Kauri's net had been able to disable the ship's propulsion systems and nudge it away from Luna City. Twelve seconds later the ship struck the surface just as Nahral Smith's ship had done. The impact obliterated the ship and its passengers and left everyone in the command station shocked at the wanton destruction of so many lives.

"Comm, where is that small runabout that departed the doomed ship before it started its descent?"

"It has established a low orbit around the equator. The heading is directly toward Luna City."

"Keep an eye on him. I suspect Joseph Warren is aboard. It's too small a craft to carry more than 15 to 18 people. I expect he and whoever is with him will be heavily armed. When he gets within 40 kilometers of Luna City let me know."

Next, Jax commed Andie at Aitken Mine.

"Andie, we may have a little trouble coming our way in the form of Joseph Warren. I believe he left his ship before it plowed into the surface. Take one of the shuttles and bring 100 of your best team members to my command center now."

"You got it, Jax. We'll be there within twenty minutes. Flannigan out."

Jax's main concern was Joseph Warren. Did he leave the ship before it crashed? It was hard for Jax to imagine he would allow his ship to crash while onboard. It was more likely he programmed the ship to

133

crash, then left with a small contingent of mercenaries. He must somehow believe he could still inflict damage on Jax and the Lunatics that were intent on becoming an independent world. Both Warren, if he maintained his present speed and heading, and Andie would arrive at about the same time. Jax decided to have a large force meet one or both of them on the landing pad as they arrived. He would do everything he could to stop any more killings. What Warren wanted was another matter. Jax knew he had to disarm the man before he did any more damage.

CHAPTER TWENTY-ONE

Andie was as good as her word. Her team arrived twenty-two minutes after Jax commed her. The shuttle was just touching down when the comm turned to Jax.

"Sir, the small runabout is now within 40 kilometers of the city."

"Thanks, comm."

Jax switched frequencies and contacted Andie as well as the team he had sent to the landing pads.

"This is Escobar. Warren will be here within a few minutes. Wait for Warren's ship to touch down then take him into custody. Then we can find out what the man wants."

"Sir, this is Flannigan. Four auto-controlled ore freighters are due to touch down over the next twelve minutes. We should clear the landing pads as quickly as possible. They can't be stopped from landing and the wash from the engines could injure any of us out there when they arrive."

"Right, Flannigan. We'll clear the pads just as soon as our friend Warren arrives. Escobar out."

Joseph Warren was prepared to take over the control room at Tycho Base as soon as he touched down. His choice to come in under the net ensured his armaments hadn't been deactivated. He also had onboard seven high yield thermonuclear devices which he intended to activate if his plan failed. If he couldn't have the bounty of the satellite then no one would have it. He gave no thought to the loss of life his actions might cause.

"Men, when we touch down, I want everyone on the surface as quickly as possible. I'll bring up the rear as we depart the vessel and follow you to the control center."

At that moment the navigator called out to everyone aboard.

"Sir, we'll be on the landing pad in one minute."

"Hear that, men? You know what needs to be done. Get ready, there's no telling what they might throw at us."

The ship landed and Warren's team was on the lunar surface in moments. Warren was surprised there were no immediate offensive actions from Escobar and his team.

"Spread out, men. You know what to do. I don't know what to expect from this rabble so be prepared for anything."

Then, over his helmet comm, Joseph Warren heard the voice of Jason Escobar.

"Warren, this is Escobar. Get your men and your ship off the landing pad. Four automated ore freighters are coming in and you are all in danger. Put down your weapons and get to the airlock as soon as possible. Do you understand?"

"I don't believe anything you're saying, Escobar. My men are here to regain legitimate control of this base and all of the property owned and managed by LMC. Don't try to stop us."

Warren stayed near his ship while his team made their way to the airlock. Jax's team stood between them and the airlock. As they came closer together Warren's men slowed to a stop.

"Escobar, let my men enter."

"Only after they have put down their weapons. I intend to protect the citizens of Luna and this base from any intrusion from you. Put down your weapons and we will allow you to enter. Once inside we can discuss our next moves. Escobar out."

Warren's men were at an impasse. They couldn't stay on the surface indefinitely and Warren wouldn't let them back on the ship. Finally, Matthews, who had been leading the team spoke.

"Escobar, this is Matthews. I'm leading the team from LMC. Open the airlock. We'll put down our weapons, now."

The group surrounding the airlock entry all put down their weapons and stood quietly waiting for the lock to open.

As Warren watched, his rage exploded in a profusion of profanity, sputtering obscenities, and unintelligible screams. It didn't stop his team from entering the open airlock under the guard of Jax's team and waiting as the door closed and the lock cycled. Warren decided the only thing he could do was set off one or more of his bombs. He turned to his ship but the navigator, and the only man left on board, had closed the bay door to protect himself from the exhaust of the incoming cargo ships. As he continued screaming at his navigator, his team, and Escobar, he didn't notice the first of four cargo vessels clear the short horizon and begin its descent onto the surface. As it approached Escobar tried to warn him."

"Warren, get out of there. The ship you see will be landing in less than a minute and anyone on the pad will be exposed to the exhaust from its engines. Head for our airlock, now."

Warren was beyond caring. He started working the manual override to the cargo bay but it required a deft hand in an environment in which he had never worked. The light gravity didn't let him get the torque he needed to slowly move the door open. Before he knew it, it was too late.

The cargo ship began to hover over the pad next to Warren's ship and its exhaust was aimed directly at the lunar surface. The wash began to push the ship around. Warren's suit began to melt and the faceplate shattered. Before his breath was taken away by the vacuum and over-heated exhaust, he only had time to look toward Tycho Base control. Then, the superheated exhaust simply consumed his body.

In the control room, Jason watched as the man responsible for so much that was wrong on the moon was destroyed.

Jax looked in stunned silence as the cargo ship settled onto the landing pad. No one else in the room moved either. Then, knowing he needed to secure the city and base he turned to Flannigan.

"Who's in charge of LMC now?"

"Back on Earth, it must be someone on the board of directors. None of us up here are part of the management group. Well, maybe Tebaldi is part of that group."

"Good, Andie. Get him up here right now."

When Tebaldi arrived Jax stood right in his face.

"Warren is dead. His troops are disabled and we are in control. I'm returning you and the troopers that landed with Warren back to Earth on one of those ore freighters out there. Luna is independent, now, and you're not welcome."

"You and the rabble here can't do that. LMC has invested too much money to simply turn this asset over to you and the local population."

"You'll have to read the declaration Lunar Freedom has released. In it, the moon becomes a self-governed world and the citizens will benefit from the wealth that comes from within. LMC will be reimbursed for the infrastructure over time but the Lunatics will be the recipients of the products taken from the moon and created on the moon."

"You can't do that, Escobar. LMC is the legal owner and won't give up this asset without a fight."

"A fight is what they will have. We've already heard from seven outposts that are joining us in our revolution. LMC is done for. It won't take long for the Earth to recognize us as an independent world. If not immediately, then certainly when we stop trading with them. There are enough moons, colonies, and outposts to give us the trade we need to survive."

"LMC won't allow this to stand. They will send an even larger force to retake the mines and subdue the populace. They'll haul you and your cohorts back to Earth and put you on trial."

"Maybe not. We've sent messages to the colonies and other mining sites. They should recognize us as independent. Once that happens, you're done. I'm sending you back to Earth on one of the ore freighters that just landed. They are scheduled to depart in four hours. We're keeping the *Mademoiselle Rouge*."

"That's outright theft. You can't do that. Besides, none of the colonies you've reached out to have responded. They may align with LMC. Then your little revolt will be over and the moon will once again be part of LMC." "Don't be so sure. Titan, Mars and Ganymede have acknowledged our message and have taken the matter under consideration. It's only a matter of time. You participated in an unprovoked attack on our satellite. Call our capture of the Rouge reparations.. Now, get out of my sight."

Tebaldi's demeanor suddenly changed and he stepped slightly closer to Jax. In a soft and silky voice, he said,

"I could make life very interesting for you. Together we could rule the known galaxy. You would also have the added benefit of my constant companionship. As lovers, we would be unstoppable."

Jax leaned even closer and said,

"I would rather sleep with fourteen rattlesnakes than have you in my bed. Andie, take him to the brig until it's time to send him back to Earth. Also, instruct the remaining LMC vessels to return to Earth now. We're done here."

As Tebaldi exited the control center Martin Kauri walked in with a broad smile on his face.

"We did it, boss. The moon is ours. There's a flood of communication from all over the system. Their messages convey their support. Recognition of our independence should come shortly." He hugged Jax and then kissed him long and hard.

"It's time we became Prime One to each other. What do you say?"

"Martin, you got me into this and I'm glad we've saved the moon for the Lunatics. I guess you're right. It is time we became one."

The two kissed again, then turned to the view screen overlooking the landing pads. Warren's ship had just lifted off and the dust was settling over the field. Crews had started loading the ore carriers and lift off would occur on schedule.

"Rho."

"Aye, sir."

"Notify everyone the satellite is secure. Have them stand down and return to regular duties. Keep the team on alert in case there are any further developments. That's all."

He turned again to Martin and hugged him even closer.

"It never crossed my mind I would fall in love with a hunk of rock and a hunk of a man at the same time. Kiss me, you Lunatic."

The End

www.ingramcontent.com/pod-product-compliance
Lightning Source LLC
Chambersburg PA
CBHW030130260626
47156CB00008B/2874